Murder in Miniature

And Other Stories

Compiled and Introduced
by Barry Pike

ACADEMY
CHICAGO

Copyright © 1992 by Academy Chicago Publishers
Illustrations copyright © Barbara Ann Spann
All rights reserved

Published by Academy Chicago Publishers
An imprint of Chicago Review Press Incorporated
814 North Franklin Street
Chicago, Illinois 60610
ISBN 978-0-89733-559-1

Library of Congress Cataloging-in-Publication Data
Bruce, Leo. 1903–1980.
Murder in miniature: the short stories of Leo Bruce / com-
piled and with an introduction by B. A. Pike.
p. cm.
ISBN 0-89733-367-5 (hardcover)
ISBN-13: 978-0-89733559-1 (paperback)
1. Detective and mystery stories, English. I. Pike, B. A.
II. Title.
PR6005.R673M 87 1992
823'.912—dc20   92-46423
                              CIP

Printed in the United States of America

Contents

Murder in Miniature:
The Short Stories of Leo Bruce

⇥▶▮◀ Introduction

When, recently, Ruth Rendell began to publish
books under a pseudonym, she made it clear
from the outset that she is "Barbara Vine".
Earlier writers, however, tended not to claim
their pseudonymous work, so that "Maxwell
March" was not identified with Margery
Allingham, nor "Mary Westmacott" with Aga-
tha Christie. In the same way, "Leo Bruce",
despite the thirty-one novels and twenty-eight
stories in his name, was unacknowledged by
Rupert Croft-Cooke as his alter ego. The
Bruce canon was not mentioned in his *Who's
Who* entry and only two of his twenty-seven
volumes of autobiography make any reference to his detective fiction.[*] Even after his

---

[*]In The *Sound of Revelry* (1969) he admits to having
'published a whodunit under a pseudonym', and in *The
Green, Green Grass* (1977) he records that his secretary
has typed, among much else, 'twenty-five novels published under a pen-name'.

death the obituary in the London *Times* did not reveal the pseudonym.

Such reticence is disconcerting to students of the form, who can never know enough; but it was evidently standard practice that distinguished crime writers with more "significant" reputations elsewhere made light of their detective fiction when writing about themselves: the Coles put their politics first and "Nicholas Blake" his work as C. Day-Lewis. Few things, however, are as durable as good detective fiction. Ngaio Marsh will continue to be esteemed for her novels when her theatre productions are forgotten, and the works of Leo Bruce may well outlive those of Rupert Croft-Cooke. Ironically, it is Leo Bruce who is celebrated in the *Dictionary of Literary Biography* (and in Tokyo, where he has a fan club). Rupert Croft-Cooke now takes second place.

Some account of Leo Bruce appeared as early as 1947 in *How to Enjoy Detective Stories* by Gilbert Thomas. This book is one of a series edited by Rupert Croft-Cooke, so that the description of Bruce has a certain privy piquancy (as when Anthony Burgess reviewed a novel by "Joseph Kell" or Julian Barnes solemnly discussed on television the work of "Dan Kavanagh"). Thomas described his editor as "a witty and erudite writer with many interests . . . an authority on antique furniture and rare books and . . . an expert on gypsies and Romany lore". Anyone who knew Croft-Cooke must have recognised him from this description; as a comprehensive thumbnail sketch it is admirable.

Rupert Croft-Cooke was a stockbroker's son, born at Edenbridge in Kent on 20 June 1903 and educated at various schools, including Tonbridge and Wellington College, Salop. He became a teacher, at first in English preparatory schools but later in Buenos Aires and at Zug in Switzerland. He also sold books, initially with his younger brother, later in partnership with an antique dealer. When World War II came, he joined the Army, serving in the Intelligence Corps in Madagascar, where he earned the British Empire Medal. By the end of the war he had risen from the ranks to become a Field Security Officer in India. Otherwise, he lived by his pen, publishing in all 126 books over 55 years, the first in 1922, when he was 19, the last in 1977, two years before his death on 10 June 1979, late in his 76th year.

His books embrace a remarkable variety of forms and include, besides the detective fiction, mainstream novels, plays, poems, collections of stories, biographies, literary histories, cookery books and a range of titles on psychology, wine, the circus, darts and gypsies. He also recorded, over 27 volumes, his exhaustive autobiography. At the age of 20 he worked in Buenos Aires on a magazine called *Sport and Society*, going on to found and edit a journal, *La Estrella* (in which he "could abuse, praise, patronise whom or what" he pleased). Later, in London, he contributed to *G.K's Weekly*, *The New Coterie*, *Theatre World*, *The Tablet* and *The Daily Mirror*, and from 1947, for six years, he wrote the book page for *The Sketch*. He translated two books from the Spanish, collaborated, among others, with Beverly Nichols, G.B. Stern and Peter Cotes, and edited a book of anti-Fascist essays. His literary friends included Lord Alfred Douglas, Louis Golding and Sir Compton Mackenzie, but he detested Peter Cheyney. Until he tired of them late in life, he collected books (and wrote most entertainingly about them in his autobiographies). He also collected English watercolours.

He appears to have been a compulsive travel-
ler and he lived abroad for many years, notably
in Tangier, from 1954-1969. Even at home he
loved a travelling life, whether with the Rosaire
circus family or with his gypsy friends. In 1937
he travelled through seven European countries
with two of the Rosaires, as recorded in *The
Man in Europe Street* (1938). *The Quest for
Quixote* (1959) took him to Spain and *The
Wintry Sea* (1964) is an account of a voyage
"through the Mediterranean on a Yugoslav car-
go boat during the coldest months of one of
Europe's most icy winters for a century ".

Throughout his life he was very much his own
man, something of a maverick by conventional
standards, rejecting "puritan" values and inhi-
bitions and conducting his life entirely as he
saw fit. From boyhood he was seen as trouble-
some, "a difficult son whose standards were
not the generally accepted ones". His adoles-
cence was marked by a sudden fervour for
Roman Catholicism and for recurrent crises at
school: before Wellington College, Salop finally took him on, he was removed both from
Tonbridge and its successor.

He described his life as "a thing of extremes", "followed with immense gusto through highly varied settings". By his own account, he was "not made for communal life" and attempts to make him "a conventionally respected figure" all failed. He saw himself as opposed to "the processes which seek to destroy individualism" and claimed to have made his "own kind of life in defiance of almost universally accepted standards and conventions". He regarded the forces of British puritanism as "loathsome" and "evil" (and in his early bookselling days publicly supported the novelist Norah C. James when one of her novels was "under threat of prosecution".)

In 1953 he fell foul of "the filthy-minded officialdom" and "cruel and senseless" laws of England when he was sent to jail for nine months for alleged homosexual offences. His secretary, Joseph, had invited two sailors to spend the weekend at their home. The men later ran into trouble with the police, and in the course of the investigation into their misdemeanours the charge of illicit sexual activity was brought against Croft-Cooke and Joseph. Though he persisted in his denials (and maintained them in the book he published after the event: *The Verdict of You All*, 1955), Croft-Cooke was sentenced to imprisonment and served nine months, first in Brixton and later in Wormwood Scrubs. Understandably, he left England at the first available opportunity after what he described as his "coming-out party".

Despite his 27 volumes of autobiography, Rupert Croft-Cooke remains an elusive figure. There are photos of his friends and his homes in some of his books, but there is no picture of him. The National Portrait Gallery has no portrait of him (though a caricature by Nicolas Bentley is known to exist). He claimed that the books were "not about me but about what I have seen and heard and known" and that they "avoid the deeper issues of love, religion or philosophy". His aim, he said, was to convey "what it was like to be alive at such a time." Though he documents his entire life, from his earliest years (*The Green, Green Grass*, 1977), he tends to avoid emotions other than anger and renders more of the surface than the inwardness of things: even the admission of his homosexuality is implicit rather than actual. After the trauma of his imprisonment he is forgivably savage about the society that treated him so harshly, but in general he keeps calm and remains genially detached.

"Leo Bruce" did not come into being until 1936, when *Case For Three Detectives* was published by Geoffrey Bles. The author's evident intention was to establish a coarse-grained, plebeian detective as a reaction to the fastidious patricians in vogue at that time, Lord Peter Wimsey prominent among them. This first novel makes the point decisively by allowing caricatures of Wimsey, Hercule Poirot and Father Brown to be outmanoeuvred by Sergeant Beef, the stolid village policeman. Four more Beef novels appeared over the next four years.

Beef is a marvellous character, robust and unaffected in his manners and attitudes but frequently sly and astute in the conduct of his cases. He appears to be the typical beef-witted policeman of caricature, heavy and lumbering, with a red face and a ginger moustache that trails in his beer. He speaks "the mixed and curious Cockney of the districts outside London". The pub is his natural habitat and he is "a passionate darts-player" (though "no champion": "it was his fervour that was remarkable, not his skill"). His "great quality as a detective" is "his sturdy common sense" and there is "something akin to genius" under "his solid exterior". Though a figure of fun in certain ways, he earns our respect and we never doubt his powers. After his initial success he quits the force and sets up his plate in Lilac Crescent, as near to Baker Street as his resources allow.

Throughout the series Bruce employs a narrator, the primly decorous Lionel Townsend, a nervous, inhibited soul, alternately embarrassed by Beef's crudities and emboldened by his achievements. Like Malcolm Warren in the novels of C.H.B. Kitchin, Townsend dithers on the edges of life, a spectator rather than a participator. He is also invariably wrong about the solutions to the mysteries. The contrast between his delicate temperament and Beef's forthright vigour gives the books a sturdy comic framework. The incongruous friendship is continually tested by Townsend's quivering distaste for Beef's vulgarities and by Beef's aggrieved conviction that a more resourceful narrator might win him a wider public. The persistence of this latter theme might reflect the author's frustration with his failure to achieve best sellerdom — and it is a tribute to his tenacity that he persisted nonetheless, over thirty years and through thirty-one books.

Sergeant Beef figures in eight novels and ten known stories, making his final appearance in 1952 in *Cold Blood*, much the darkest of an otherwise high-spirited series. Three years later Carolus Deene was introduced, perhaps on the principle that if you can't beat 'em, you join 'em. Where Beef was a reaction against the genteel tradition, Deene is very much within it. He is sensitive and civilised, a public schoolmaster with substantial private means, who indulges his passion for criminal investigation whenever he sees fit. He is a widower who remains detached, a cool, cynical spectator, with humanity, humour, an independent spirit and a strong, satirical intelligence. The novels in which he features are formula fiction of a very high order. Though almost obsessively conventional, they are most skillfully contrived, to amuse, intrigue, surprise and satisfy. Few crime writers ring the changes on the formal pattern so adroitly and resourcefully and yet provide so reassuringly the mixture as before. Each case is a ritual progress, from the standard attempts to deflect Carolus from involvement to the final assembly of suspects, before whom he provides the solution. He moves calmly and efficiently through twenty-three cases in all, working by instinct and logic and with minimal resort to forensic evidence. His conversational habit of enquiry involves him with a diverse host of characters, all vividly imagined and many engagingly quirky. The monotony inherent in the method is routed by the variety and vitality of these encounters and the author's gift for entertaining dialogue is everywhere apparent. So is his extraordinary gift for mystery, for teasing and tangling and contriving, with cunning and daring. As an exponent of the classic detective novel in its pure form he is unquestionably in the front rank.

The stories collected here are important on four counts. They complete, so far as is known, the oeuvre of a major detective novelist, whose slightest achievement is of interest to students and enthusiasts of the form; they add to our knowledge of Sergeant Beef, one of the most colourful of fictional detectives (and one whose full-length cases are too few in number); they introduce an unexpected third detective to the Brucean canon, the astute and resourceful policeman, Sergeant Grebe, eight of whose cases are recorded here; and they offer a last chance to encounter anew their author's characteristic wit and ingenuity.

It would be absurd to claim for them more than their author would have done at the time of their composition. They were written for a daily newspaper and their aim was to provide ephemeral diversion. Nonetheless, they are well worth rescuing from oblivion. Even the slightest is deft and telling, skillfully narrated, with economy and point. The best are worthy additions to the canon, elegant, clever and satisfying.

All but one of this collection were written for the London *Evening Standard*, where they appeared between 1950 and 1956. "On the Spot" appeared in 1951 in the short-lived magazine *Magpie*. Two stories only have been available till now in *Evening Standard* anthologies: "Clue in the Mustard" (anthologized as "Death In the Garden") and "Murder in Miniature", both featuring Sergeant Beef. The present collection assembles twenty-six further stories: eight more with Beef, the eight with Sergeant Grebe and ten with no series character. So far as is known, there are no stories featuring Carolus Deene. *Twentieth Century Crime and Mystery Writers*, edited by John Reilly (2nd edition, St James Press, 1985), incorrectly lists a twenty-ninth story, 'Bloody Moon'. Robert Adey has recently established that this story is by George Bruce and so has nothing to do with the current undertaking.

B. A. Pike
London
January, 1993

Note: Except for the quotation from Gilbert Thomas, all quotations are taken either from Rupert Croft-Cooke's autobiographical volume *The Sensual World* or from Sergeant Beef novels by Leo Bruce.

⇢▸❙◀⇠ Clue in the Mustard

"My first important case?" said Sergeant Beef. "Yes, I can tell you about that. I shouldn't hardly call it a who-done-it, though, because everybody knew that if old Miss Crackliss had been murdered, there was only one person it could be. All the same, it was an interesting case. What you'd call mackayber..."

"Mack...?"

"You know, gruesome," explained Beef impatiently.

"Oh, macabre."

"That's it."

I knew better than to underrate Sergeant Beef because of a little eccentricity in pronunciation. Large, crimson of cheek, a hearty eater and a good public bar man whose ginger moustache had refreshed itself in many a pint glass, he looked what he once had been, a village policeman. But his insight and common sense had enabled him to solve a number of murder cases, and now he had retired from the Force he was gaining a reputation as a private investigator.

The case he described to me happened twenty years ago or more, when Sergeant Beef was a constable stationed in a small village called Long Cotterell, in one of the home counties. His passions were gardening and darts; when it was too dark to continue the one he settled down nightly to the other. Then old Miss Crackliss, who lived at the Mill House, died suddenly.

He knew Miss Crackliss well. In fact, he confessed, he used to put in a few hours at the week-end helping her gardener.

"Pay wasn't so plentiful in those days," he explained, "and I wanted a bit extra to get married on. Besides, she let me put odds and ends in her greenhouse, and *that* was handy, too."

Miss Crackliss was in her sixties, a frail and shrunken old lady, who suffered from heart trouble. To look at her, Beef said, "you wouldn't have thought she'd have taken much murdering." She was reputed to be excessively rich.

Her nephew lived with her, and in the eyes of the village here was a ready-made suspect.

Ripton Crackliss was the least popular resident of Long Cotterell, a tall, gloomy man in his thirties, powerful and slow-moving; he had a way of ignoring the greetings of others.

It was understood that Ripton Crackliss would inherit everything on his aunt's death.

The Mill House stood well away from the village, a pleasant red-brick house with a walled garden beside it, in which were two large green-houses. It was in this garden that Beef was working on the last occasion on which he saw Miss Crackliss alive, a Saturday afternoon in May.

"I was off duty," he explained, "and I'd come up to do a bit of planting out for her. Besides, I had a couple of boxes of mustard and cress in the conservatory and I wanted to see how they were doing.

"I went in to look at my boxes and found the seedlings coming through nicely, then I went over to get on with her work.

"Presently the old lady came out to settle down in her garden chair for the afternoon.

"She had one of those metal-framed chairs with canvas seats and backs to them, because she liked sitting upright and not stretching out as you would in a deck-chair. I went and said good afternoon to her.

"She was all wrapped round with rugs because, although there was sunshine, it was none too warm. She seemed quite cheerful, sitting there with her book and looking up to see what I was doing. Her own gardener finished midday Saturdays. The next day I heard she was dead."

At first there seemed nothing unnatural about this, for the local doctor, a great friend of Beef's, had long been prepared for a fatal heart attack. He was a keen, conscientious man, this Doctor Ryder-Boyce, and he was upset by the event because he liked old Miss Crackliss.

It appeared that when tea-time came she had not returned to the house and the housekeeper, a stern Scotswoman called Mrs Craig, had gone up to the room which Ripton called his study and told him that his aunt was still outside.

Ripton had got up and said he would go across to the walled garden and bring her in to tea.

There was nothing unusual in this. The old lady loved her garden and was apt to stay far too long in it when the weather was not really warm enough. Besides, she frequently dozed off to sleep. So Mrs Craig made the tea. Then Ripton Crackliss came hurrying into the house.

"You must go to her at once," he said. "She's had one of her attacks, I think. I'm afraid she's dead."

Mrs Craig set out for the walled garden while Ripton telephoned for the doctor. She found Miss Crackliss dead, sitting in her chair with the blankets round her. There was a look almost of horror in the dead eyes and the features seemed somehow twisted as though with fear.

"Poor thing," thought Mrs Craig. "She must have died in pain after all. One of those terrible attacks of hers."

But she noticed something else. The dead face was flushed as she had rarely seen it.

The doctor arrived and ordered Miss Crackliss to be carried up to her bedroom. He made his examination and asked both Mrs Craig and Ripton Crackliss a number of questions. She had said nothing to lead either of them to suppose she was unwell. She had lunched with them. As Mrs Craig said, there could be nothing to upset her in anything she had eaten or drunk because all three of them had had the same.

The doctor went home, but later that afternoon he telephoned to Beef and suggested that he should come round.

Beef found the doctor silent and abstracted.

"Know what they're saying in the village?" he asked. "They think Ripton Crackliss did for his aunt this afternoon."

"What makes them think that?" asked the doctor.

"Well, you know what gossip is. They don't like the fellow and they know he gets her money. Besides, he was up at the house all the afternoon. Think there's anything in it?"

"I don't see how there can be," said the doctor. "I've examined the old lady and she certainly died as a result of her heart trouble. It might have come at any time, as you know. The fact that she seemed well to-day means nothing."

"Then what are you so worried about?" asked Beef.

"I simply can't say. Yet there is something I don't like about it. She *looked* strange, for one thing. As though she'd had a shock—from the outside, I mean. And there were a couple of points. . ."

"Go on," said Beef.

"They may mean nothing at all. Probably they

don't. But I'm not quite happy."

"What were these points?"

"Just above her upper lip was a tiny smudge. At first I thought it was dirt, but it was sticky. Only a very small smudge. But she never ate sweets."

"And the other one?"

"When the three of us went out to carry her in, Ripton Crackliss got there first and seemed to be trying to drag her to her feet. He'd got hold of her forearms and was pulling quite hard. When I examined her later I found that he had been so violent that it had left marks on the skin. It seemed such an extraordinary thing to do when we were all on our way to carry her properly."

"Yes," said Beef. "There were no signs of violence?"

"None at all. Not even an abrasion any-where."

"And she could not have been poisoned?"

"That, of course, we shall find out if I'm not satisfied. But I see no signs of it at all."

"I think I'll go and have a look round that garden, though," said Beef. "It won't be dark for another couple of hours yet."

Beef cycled off to the Mill House. Putting his cycle into the hedge, he went straight to the walled garden. The chair in which Miss Crackliss had sat that afternoon was still there, and he examined it carefully. Then he made a minute inspection of the rough stone paving on which it had stood.

"There was nothing," he said, telling me the story. "Nothing at all in the way of a clue. I decided to pack up and wait for the post-mortem, if there was going to be one."

Before he started for home he thought he would go and have a look at his mustard and cress, and switched the light on in the greenhouse. This brought Ripton Crackliss over from the house at a run, and he asked Beef what the hell he was doing. Beef remained calm.

"I'm just having a look at my seedlings," he said. "Come on wonderfully, haven't they?"

Ripton Crackliss seemed to control his anger.

"I understand that you had permission from my aunt to use this place," he said. "But my aunt died this afternoon. In future, if you want to come here please call at the house first and see if it's convenient."

"Very well, sir," said Beef, and followed him

out.

He went straight back to the doctor's house and the two talked seriously for half an hour. Then they got into the doctor's car and drove off to the nearby town. Here they went to the police station and another conference took place. Within forty-eight hours a warrant was out for the arrest of Ripton Crackliss on a charge of murdering his aunt.

"Caused quite a sensation at the time," said Beef, "and I won't say it didn't do me a bit of good in the Force. 'Murder in the Garden', the papers called it, but that was wrong, because the murder hadn't taken place in the garden at all."

"No?"

"No. It was in the greenhouse. You know what that fellow had done? He'd waited till his aunt was in her chair, tucked up tight in her rugs so that she couldn't move in a hurry, then he'd come out to her.

"Must have been about two o'clock that Sunday afternoon when Mrs Craig was having her nap and nobody would have seen him going across from the house. All of a sudden he'd put a piece of plaster, like they use for bandages, over her mouth and held her arms to the chair.

"What could she do? She was a frail little thing and couldn't even struggle enough to leave any traces. Then he'd tied her arms to the framework of the chair and she was powerless.

"Of course, it needed more than that. Doesn't matter how weak and old people are, they don't die easily. He lifted the chair with her on it and took it across to the greenhouse. He had the furnace stoked up and the heat in there was the maximum.

"That's what killed her. With her heart she was dead an hour later—or sooner, let's hope."

"Good Lord," I couldn't help exclaiming.

"I told you it was gruesome. But ingenious, too. She really had died of a heart attack and there might have been no evidence of anything else.

"He'd thought about the marks of where her arms were tied and covered that up by pretending to try to pull her out of her chair when we went across with the doctor.

"We got quite a lot of evidence, but I doubt even then whether he would have been hanged if he hadn't confessed.

"There was the mark of the sticking plaster,

and the fact that a whole sack of coke had been used after the gardener left on Saturday. And he was the only one on the spot. But he might have got off for lack of medical evidence. You see, the way he had chosen left no trace at all. Murder by heat, you might call it."

"But what gave you the idea?" I asked him. "What really led you to see what had happened?"

He smiled slowly.

"It was that mustard and cress of mine," he said. "I told you I said to Ripton Crackliss that it had come on wonderfully. Well, it had. It had shot up. And there had been no sun that day.

"As soon as I saw those long, thin stalks I knew there was something wrong. That was my only clue."

➼➤❚❰❮ Holiday Task

Sitting on the rocks under some of the highest cliffs on the coast of Normandy I watched Sergeant Beef deliberately enjoying his holiday. With a floppy canvas hat on his head and trousers rolled up to the knee, he was prawning.

The sun was high when Beef proposed that we should go up the cliff path for a drink and I readily agreed. We were crossing the beach when to my surprise he hailed one of three men approaching us.

"It's old Léotard," he said aside to me. "One of the best detectives in the Sûrété. I worked with him on the Mr G. case. Hullo, Leo!"

"It is my friend Beef!" he said in English, and a string of introductions followed.

Beef, redundant as ever, had to explain that he was on holiday, and Léotard said that he wished he were. He was very much on a job.

"Body washed up?" Beef grinned.

"No, no," said the Frenchman with a half smile. "Not washed up. Cast down."

"What, off the cliff?"

"You come and see if you like," Léotard invited, and we all moved off in the direction in which the Frenchman had been going when Beef hailed him.

Léotard explained a little as we went. That morning some boys had reported the wreckage of a car at the foot of the tall cliff known as the White Bear, and a policeman had gone down to investigate.

He had found that "wreckage" was a mild word to use for the shattered bits of metal which were all that remained of a Renault car. He had also found a corpse.

"Identified yet?" asked Beef.

"Oh yes," said Léotard. "It hid the body of a M. Henri Poinsteau, the newly appointed governor of the largest prison in Normandy, and reputed to be the most detested man in the French prison service."

"Ah!" exclaimed Beef.

"Not 'ah,' my dear friend. There is no 'ah' that we can find. The car was Poinsteau's. It had been driven at speed straight over the cliff edge—a case of suicide."

"Daresay you're right," conceded Beef. "It's not the way I'd choose, though. You know his reason for it, I suppose?"

"Not yet. The case was only reported this morning. I arrived an hour ago. The body, or what was left of it, was, of course, photographed, measurements taken of its situation and drawings made before it was removed."

We were approaching a tangle of metal and upholstery which had once been a car.

"We must see what we can now," said Léotard, "for in another hour the tide will be in."

The third man began taking fingerprints, and Léotard himself examined the beach near by. Beef scarcely glanced at the wreckage or the beach but kept gazing up at the cliff-head above us. He was the first to speak.

"I don't believe this was suicide," he announced.

"We shall see," snapped Léotard.

During the next few days Sergeant Beef continued to spend his mornings prawning and to eat gargantuan meals at our little hotel. But in the evenings he and Léotard seemed to enjoy talking shop, and I listened.

If Beef was right in his almost psychic dismissal of the suicide theory and consequent belief that Poinsteau had been murdered, then, admitted Léotard, it would not be hard to find motives. In the criminal world he had countless bitter enemies, men who had suffered from his savagery and sadism.

But beyond this admission Léotard would not go. He could see nothing connected with the death which could be called evidence of murder.

The finger-prints found on the steering wheel were Poinsteau's and the car expert believed that the engine was running when the car hit the ground. It seemed certain that Poinsteau had driven himself over the edge of the cliff.

But why? Nothing that Léotard could learn about the dead man gave any indication of this. He was a bachelor who lived alone; his financial affairs were in order and he appeared to enjoy his position. Besides, he had just been appointed to one of the most important posts in the service.

"He only moved in on the day before the body was found," explained Léotard. "He had spent the afternoon in supervising the arrangement of his furniture which had just arrived from his last quarters. He had some fine furniture, large Empire pieces, and they suited the new house admirably.

"He had arrived at the prison in his car at lunch time and all the afternoon he had been with the moving men, while his car had been in the garage which adjoins his house. Later that evening he must have decided to go for a drive, for when one of his assistants came to his house he found that Poinsteau was not at home, and the garage empty."

Beef nodded.

"You have one advantage," he told Léotard. "Its happening in a prison makes it easy for you to check up times, and so on. The gatekeeper must have seen him go out. What time was it?"

Léotard frowned.

"Now we come to a rather funny thing," he said. "The gatekeeper swears he never did come out. He was on duty from twelve noon till midnight. He remembers Poinsteau arriving in his car, but he is quite certain that he had not left when he went off duty.

"The man who took his place says the same. Poinsteau's was the only car in the prison pre-mises, and it did not pass the gate that evening."

"That's odd," said Beef. "What other ways out are there?"

"None," said Léotard. "Of that you can be certain. There is no other exit from the jail."

"Then," I put in, "if Poinsteau was murdered it must have been a widespread plot in which one of the gatekeepers was involved. Perhaps his murderers came from the inside, drove him to the cliff's edge in his own car and pushed him over."

"Or murdered him first," suggested Léotard, "and merely set the engine running with a corpse at the wheel. The injuries were such that no one could possibly tell if he had been killed by a blow on the head, for instance.

"But the trouble with that theory is that the two gatekeepers are most reliable men who seem to be speaking the truth. His subordinates in the service for the most part respected Poinsteau. It was the prisoners who hated him."

It amused me to notice how absorbed Beef had become in this case.

He seemed able to think and talk of little else but the rival theories of suicide and murder, weighing the points in favor of each. So far as

Léotard's investigations went, there was no motive for suicide, for it had been found that the dead man had no money worries and the most persistent inquiries could not bring to light any private intrigue or complication.

On the other hand, for murder there were plenty of motives, and suspects as well. The chief obstacle to the murder theory was the fact that Poinsteau must have somehow driven through the gates himself, or have left his car outside the prison earlier in the day — at all events made a voluntary exit.

Unless the gatekeepers were involved it seemed impossible that the murderers, however many or however powerful they may have been, should have spirited the governor and his car from a closely guarded prison.

Then, a few days before our holiday would end, Léotard made an exciting discovery. Two men who had served long sentences under Poinsteau had arrived in the nearest large town a fortnight before the governor's death and left on the morning after it. Léotard had a dossier for each of them and they were certainly well qualified as suspects. The elder one, known as The Ace, had been sentenced for manslaughter and the younger for robbery with violence.

They were both sworn enemies of Poinsteau and the younger brother of The Ace was doing a sentence of three years' hard labour in the jail to which Poinsteau had been appointed and would have come under his authority that day.

Besides, the movements of the two men had been secretive during their time in the town and too many curious people were eager to swear that they had never left a certain dockland café on the night of Poinsteau's disappearance.

"But how can I arrest them?" demanded Léotard. "Nothing to connect them with the crime."

Next morning I again accompanied Beef on his prawning expedition. Beef had just lowered all his nets when I heard him shouting excited-ly.

"What was it that Greek said?" he yelled.

"Which Greek?"

"The one that jumped out of his bath because he'd just thought of what he ought to have seen years before."

"Eureka," I told him.

"Well, that's me. Come on!"

I knew him in this mood and meekly watched

and followed while he threw his prawns back into the sea, left his nets at a café near the cliff-head, and without waiting to change his highly informal clothes sat himself in the only car in the village which was for hire and told me to get the driver to take him to Rennes.

When we approached the city I asked where he wanted to go. He consulted his notes and mispronounced the name of a firm of removal and storage contractors. I gave it to the driver and after some dangerous swerves through the streets we drew up at an office door.

"You wait here," Beef said, "unless they don't talk English, in which case I'll call you."

It seemed that there were no language difficulties, for Beef was absent some twenty minutes. When he joined me to drive home, I tackled him.

"Was that the firm which moved Poinsteau's furniture?" I asked, rather unnecessarily as I thought. But Beef had a surprise for me.

"No," he said, and closed his eyes.

When we were back he hurried to Léotard's hotel.

"Of course," was his greeting, "we ought to have seen it days ago. I must be slipping. You can arrest your two men. You'll have to fill in the details, Leo, because after all I'm on holiday, but I don't think you'll have much difficulty.

"I've just been over to see the people you told me had the order to move Poinsteau's furniture. Well, they didn't."

"Didn't have the order?"

"No. Didn't move it. They got a telephone message saying the job was off. See it now? Who else had access to him that afternoon? Who could come in and out without anyone thinking twice? The two moving men, of course. I think your gatekeeper will pick them out in any identification parade.

"Easy for them to kill Poinsteau and leave the jail as quietly and comfortably as you please. Easy for those two men to hire a van from somewhere else—or even buy one if they were in funds and determined enough. Easy job altogether."

"I am sure that it was," said Léotard. "No difficulty at all in cracking Poinsteau on the head. And then, I suppose," the Frenchman had grown very sarcastic, "the dead man sat in his car, passed the gatekeeper, went to the cliff and was still at the wheel when the car went over?"

Beef did not smile.

"Yes," he said. "That's just what happened."

Léotard prolonged the game.

"The gatekeeper could not see him because he was already a ghost, perhaps?"

"No, Leo," said Beef seriously. "The gatekeeper couldn't see him for the same reason that nobody else could. Him or his car.

"I can't think why I never thought of it before—perhaps it seems funny to have one car inside another. Yes, that's what they did. Drove it, with the corpse and all, straight up a couple of planks into the pantechnicon. That's how the governor left his prison in his own car—like Jonah in the whale's belly.

"Now you fill in the bits and pieces and go and catch your men. I want some prawns for tea."

❧ Murder in Miniature

"It's not often," said Sergeant Beef after a long pull at his pint of mild-and-bitter, "that a case falls into your lap."

I knew that behind his bovine front, his ginger moustache and heavy manner, my old friend had one of the shrewdest brains in modern detection and had solved some of the trickiest cases of our time. So I gave him the encouragement he needed.

"What do you mean — falls into your lap?"

"What I say. And it didn't half give me a crack across the knees, either. In a train, it was. I was sitting there minding my own business, alone in a third-class carriage, when wallop, the train jerks and I find myself holding a corpse that's fallen out of the luggage-rack. And one of the strangest corpses you've ever seen, too. Two foot six, he was. You remember the case? I got more publicity from it than from any other murder mystery I ever handled. You see, it was the corpse of Little Mumbo which fell into my lap, the most famous midget in the world. It was up to me then to find out who had murdered him."

A long, thoughtful silence fell on the sergeant, and I realised with a jolt that it was time to fill our glasses.

"I was just thinking," he continued. "How useful it is to be the kind of detective I am. Ex-policeman. Ordinary sort of chap. None of your ritzy types with titles and private incomes. I'm a public bar man, and if I hadn't been I might never have cleared up this case I'm telling you about. I shouldn't have had the right friends, for one thing. I shouldn't have known old Dick Sowerby who was in charge of the left-luggage office at St Watercross Station. However, I'll tell you the story as it happened.

"Little Mumbo was a rich man. Charles Mumby, his real name was, and he was a perfect midget, tiny, but wonderful proportions. He'd appeared in the big American circuses and, in fact, all over the world. Five years before this happened he had married an English girl called Nina, who was of normal size. Nothing unusual about that, I'm told. Midgets marry non-midgets more often than not, and Nina was a lovely girl. They were described by everyone who knew them as a most devoted couple. They organised their lives very cleverly so that Mumbo's midgetism shouldn't embarrass either of them, and, of course, they were rich enough to be able to do this. They had a flat in London and a house down at Southbourne, and although neither of them could drive a car they had a chauffeur and a big saloon which had a seat specially put in for the little fellow.

"I was coming up from Southbourne myself on an early train which was non-stop to London when this thing happened. Gave me a nasty shock, I can tell you. I had only just moved to that empty carriage and had not noticed the luggage rack. He was as dead as a doornail, but I recognised him at once. Before I pulled the communication cord or anything I made a quick examination of his body to see if I could find the cause of his death. There was a lot of bandaging over the left shoulder, which made me think — and the doctors proved later I was right — that he'd been stabbed there. Quickest way down to the heart, you know. It didn't need much of a blade to reach his heart, poor little fellow. Someone had done it with one easy blow. But it hadn't gone through his clothes. He had been bandaged and dressed again after he was dead.

"When we got into London there was a devil's own fuss over the corpse. Police, ambulance, everything in no time, it seemed. I was quite impressed. The reporters were on the station in a very short while and looking for the man who had found the body. But I wasn't interested in telling my story then. I wanted to find out first who had done it. So what did I do?"

Beef loved a rhetorical question, but I knew better than to try and answer it and shook my head in bewilderment.

"I watched to see whether anyone had come to meet him. No one else thought of that. They were all too busy trying to get a glimpse of the corpse. I was rewarded, all right. I saw an anxious-looking girl standing at the barriers long after all the passengers had gone and staring down the platform.

"'Excuse me,' I said. 'Were you by any chance expecting Mr Charles Mumby?'

"'Yes! Yes! Where is he?' She sounded very

near hysterical already and I wondered how I was going to break it to her. 'I'm his wife.'

"'I've got some bad news for you,' I said. 'Better come and sit down while I tell you.' It was just as well I did that because she would have fainted clean away if she'd been standing up when I told her what had happened. As it was, she gave a sort of half-scream and then started to cry. I just sat there and waited, feeling pretty bad myself, because there was nothing much a stranger could do in the circumstances.

"Presently she pulled herself together and began to tell me what had happened. Mumbo had been down Southbourne on his own for a few days. Nothing unusual in that, she said. He liked being alone sometimes and had rooms there which were fitted up to make everything easy for him. She had stayed in town and had meant to join him today, but yesterday evening she had received a phone call from him asking her to meet the 9:18 train at St Watercross Station in London next morning. He had sounded a little upset, she thought, but when she asked if anything was the matter he had said 'no' cheerfully enough. 'I wasn't really worried,' she said. 'Charlie often changed his mind. I did rather wonder why he had not come up by car, because he had it down there, and Seboys, our chauffeur. But I just came to meet the train as he said and it wasn't until he didn't appear that I began to fret. There was one strange thing, though. Seboys was on that train this morning.'

"Of course that interested me. Seboys had been one of the first to pass the barrier and had spoken to Mrs Mumby, explaining that the car had broken down and he had come to get a spare part. He hadn't noticed Mr Mumby on the train, he said, but as he had hurried on at the last moment this was not surprising. He had not waited then.

"'Did you see anyone else you knew get off the train?' I asked her.

"She hesitated over that, then said very quietly that she thought, only thought, that she had recognized Percy Mumby, Charles's brother. She was not sure, because she had not seen Percy for years. He was of normal size — Charles had been the only midget in his family — and 'not much good' it appeared. If ever he came near his little brother it was because he wanted to borrow money. Nina had seen him at their wedding and once since, she thought. What he was doing on that train she couldn't imagine. So, of course, I sent her to the police with the whole of her story. Couldn't keep evidence of that sort to myself.

"You should have seen the newspapers that day. I've never seen such headlines for a murder case. 'Little Mumbo Murdered', they said, or 'Midget Slain on Southborne Express'. Caused the biggest stir in crime for years and years. But I still kept out of it. 'A passenger discovered the body', they said, and I left it at that. I was biding my time."

Again Beef paused, this time to pick his teeth.

"It was a horrible case," he reflected. "Far more horrible than it may appear. I thought I could see daylight, but I couldn't be sure yet. There was just one thing which had given me certain suspicions, one bit of inconsistency I suppose you'd call it. I've told it to you, but I don't suppose you've noticed it. It wasn't much to go on, but it had made me think. Then when I heard that Percy Mumby had been on that train and was Suspect Number One to the police, I decided to find him.

"He was in a terribly jumpy state. Living in a little Bloomsbury hotel expecting to be arrested any minute. He *had* been down to see his brother; he had been given some money and even been told that he would inherit a large sum under Charles Mumby's will. He had no idea that his brother was on the same train that morning and travelled on it by sheer coincidence, though he did not expect ever to convince anyone of that.

"'I don't believe you did it, Mr. Mumby,' I told him.

"'Why not?' he asked at once.

"'Because I think I know who did.'

"We talked it over for some time and in the end he agreed to retain my services. I was to get evidence to prove my suspect guilty and if I was successful he would pay my fee. If I wasn't he would probably be hanged a pauper, so I should not get it. I've taken on cases like that before.

"The first thing I did was go down to Southborne. I got permission to look through the Mumby home there, but found nothing of interest at all. I had not expected to, really. I could see by now that this was a cleverly planned murder and that the guilty party was not one to leave spare clues lying about. Then I interviewed the ticket-collector at Southborne Station who had been on duty at the entrance that morning. Just as I thought, he was ready to swear that Little Mumbo had not come through his barrier. How could he have helped noticing him? he asked. Yes, there had been lots of children, babes in arms, and a couple of perambulators for the goods van. But no midgets. I came back to London feeling all the more sure that I was on the right lines.

"The police had got several new suspects, I gathered, including a man who had been confined in a mental home for some time and was on the train that morning and another man who had once worked for Little Mumbo as a dresser and could give no satisfactory account of his movements at the relevant times. The dead midget's will might have been drafted to increase their confusion, for although the bulk of the money went to the widow, the brother, the chauffeur and the dresser were all left sums large enough to provide the motive.

"It looked as though I was stumped for lack of evidence. And very soon Percy Mumby was

arrested and charged with murder, and I knew I
had to act quickly. It was then that my friendship with old Dick Sowerby came in useful.
We'd played many a game of darts together at
the Unicorn, a little pub round the back of the
station, and old Dick, a quiet, steady chap, grey
as a badger and stooping a bit, was mustard on
the double top and the sixty. I waited until we'd
won a couple of games together, then I told him
what I wanted to do. At first he shook his head
and said it would lose him his job, but I managed to talk him round. That evening, when he
was on duty alone in the left-luggage office, I
went across there and we turned up the register.

"I suppose you've guessed what I was looking
for? I wanted to examine any bag or parcel left
on the morning of my discovery of the murder.
According to my theory there had to be one,
and sure enough, there was. All the other bags
left there had been collected except a little case
which was small enough for anyone to have
carried. It was locked, but only with the ordinary kind of small key and we soon had it open.
And when old Dick saw what was inside, even
he let out a whistle and stood staring down at it
— a baby's clothes. Then I turned them over

and realised that I really was in luck because there was something else which I'd scarcely hoped to find. It was a Commando knife; one of the early models made by the Wilkinson Sword Company.

"I left Dick Sowerby there and rushed off to the Yard, so that within an hour they had collected the bag and handed the knife over to the fingerprint boys. By ten o'clock next morning Nina Mumby had been charged with the murder of her husband and I was holding a sort of press conference—more like an American president than an English police sergeant.

"Plain as a pikestaff, of course. She'd had enough of being married to that little freak. She'd worked it out nicely. Waited till he was alone at Southbourne and she alone in London with no one to know their movements at either end. She'd gone down there the night before with everything ready and stabbed Little Mumbo in his bath that morning. I don't suppose he bled much, poor little fellow, and it was all carried away by the bathwater. Then she staunched the wound and fixed it up with a bandage and dressed him in his ordinary clothes first and covered him with baby clothes over the top, seeing that his face was out of sight. She found a carriage to herself on the train, which was not very difficult because people avoid travelling with babies, and in any case that train from Southbourne is never very full on a morning early in the week. All she had to do then was to whip off the baby clothes and leave him on the rack rolled in sacking, as he was when I found him. She had a first-class ticket, I daresay, and when she had stuffed the baby clothes into her case she went along the corridor and inconspicuously took her place in a carriage near the front of the train. Then, one of the first off, she had time to take her case to the left-luggage office and be back at the barrier, an anxious wife waiting for her husband.

"Really she took very few chances. A mother with a baby at Southbourne would not be noticed sufficiently to be identified afterwards, and certainly no London ticket-collector is going to be aware that she had passed through and come back to meet the train. As soon as the talk and trouble was over she would have come and reclaimed her case, which would have attracted no attention in the meantime. After she had left me at the station she probably went home to arrange that her bed should look slept in before her char or someone came to the flat. It was a neat, workmanlike job and she might have got away with it if I hadn't noticed one very odd thing."

"And that?" I asked, since the question was only too clearly expected of me.

"Why, that she was there at all," said Beef. "At the barrier, I mean. All the passengers had long since left the train, as I told you. If she had genuinely expected her husband she would have supposed that he had missed his train or something ten minutes before. Only if she wanted to be seen there would she have waited till I found her. You might say her other mistake was to keep the knife, and certainly it was the most damning evidence at her trial. I don't see how she could have got rid of it before, though. If it had all gone according to plan she need never have worried. But how was she to know that I should be on the same train? *That* was her downfall!"

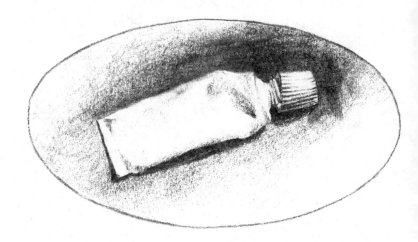

⇢⊁⊀⇠ The Doctor's Wife

"There are cases of murder," said my old friend Sergeant Beef, "in which the local man, the village bobby if you like, has all the clever boys from the Yard beaten before they start.

"They may have their microscopes and their post-mortems—he has his knowledge of the people concerned, ordinary human knowledge, which is sometimes worth all their scientific theories put together."

After this sententious preamble I expected a straightforward story, and in a way, I suppose I got it.

There was just such a case (said Beef) when I was working at a town called Braxham.

It concerned the death of a doctor's wife. And it took me right into the middle of medical terms and technicalities so that I began to feel like a doctor myself. I was talking about culture plates and bacilli for weeks afterwards.

But, mind you, I learned it all right. When you've got to be technical you've got to be, and I wasn't to be put off by any medical mumbo-jumbo.

There were several doctors in the town, but the ones we all thought most of were two partners, who were also cousins, Dr Markwright and Dr Gudge. They made a fine pair because, although both were clever and both were liked, it was generally said that Dr Gudge was the cleverer and Dr Markwright the more popular.

I don't think anyone could have denied that, for Dr Markwright was a big white-haired man who looked rather like a more amiable Mr Gladstone, and had helped lots of people for nothing and would sit up all night with a patient. Dr Gudge, who was narrow-headed and quick-moving, was known to have been proved right even when his opinion went against that of specialists.

It was Dr Markwright's wife who died. She was as nice and good-natured a woman as you could want to meet and had not an enemy in the world. She died quite naturally, it seemed, of tetanus which had set in to a wound in her hand. She had been opening a tin of peas with one of those old-fashioned tin openers and it had slipped and cut a nasty rip right down the side of her left thumb.

Dr Markwright was out on his rounds at the time and as Dr Gudge was away on holiday there was a locum in his place who was in the surgery when the little accident happened. Mrs Markwright did not wish to disturb him so she went to the small medicine cupboard which was in the room she shared with her husband.

This was for their personal use and contained the usual medicaments: cascara, aspirin, ointment, iodine, liver salts, cough mixture and whatnot, as well as bandages and plaster. Mrs Markwright's cut was too deep for iodine so she washed it carefully, and bound it up with ointment and lint until her husband would come home and attend to it properly.

The young locum was a rather dressy and conceited young man whom nobody liked very much, but I knew him as a decent dart-thrower and a man who had nothing against a pint of beer. He seemed very put out by the whole business.

Dr Markwright told his wife that she had done

quite right and renewed the same dressing. Neither of them said much about it and during the next forty-eight hours Mrs Markwright was satisfied that the little wound was healing nicely.

On the third day, however, she began to feel pain in the muscles of her legs and grew irritable, which was unusual for her. She went up to bed and said she did not want to see anyone, but when her husband went to her he found that her legs were drawn up in what he afterwards described as tonic spasms.

He realised at once what the danger was and rushed down to his surgery for anti-tetanus serum which he injected. This was of no avail and his wife died twelve hours later after violent spasms.

Dr Markwright behaved in the most heart-broken way and everyone felt the deepest sympathy with him. Moreover his conduct seemed exemplary.

Although both he and the locum agreed that his wife's death had been due to tetanus and were prepared to sign the death certificate to this effect, Dr Markwright asked that in the circumstances there should be a post-mortem examination to confirm their diagnosis.

There was, and it did so. The doctor's wife had died through a cut in her hand. But no blame attached to anyone.

And there the matter would have rested if I, a local police sergeant, had not known the parties to it, and if I had not started by having a pretty good guess at what had happened.

They say a good detective never goes on guess-work. Of course he doesn't. But half the successful investigations that have been were started by what was little more than a guess and was later substantiated.

I daresay if I wanted to give myself importance I could call that guess of mine reasoning, and say that I looked in the only direction where there was motive. But I don't like pretence. I started with a guess and then did the reasoning and investigation which proved I was right.

First of all I went up to London where no one could know anything about the case, and had a long talk with a doctor friend of mine. At the end of it I think I knew as much about tetanus as he did.

Then I got hold of all the drugs in that cupboard and sent them off to a bacteriologist. Finally I made inquiries in the town to know when the last case of tetanus had been.

That did not take long to find out. A little girl playing in a quarry about six months before had cut her knee on some loose glass and Dr Markwright had been called in too late to do anything for her. In fact, one of the things I learned was that once this strange disease is established there's almost nothing that can be done for the patient.

I asked Dr Markwright about the little girl and he seemed to be as open about it as about his own wife.

"The symptoms were similar, of course," he told me, "but in that case they took longer to develop."

"You are certain that in the little girl's case it was tetanus?" I asked.

"Oh, absolutely. I sent portions of the wound over to Dr Prince, who is a keen bacteriologist. He confirmed me at once."

I thanked him, and my next call was on Dr Prince. He remembered the case perfectly. Markwright had been most interested and he had been able to clear up all doubt.

Clever chap, Markwright. Perhaps not Gudge's brilliance but still clever. Gudge was a genius in his way. Could be a first-rate bacteriologist himself. Great friend of Prince's —often here. Markwright? Yes, but more seldom.

I asked next if I could see the culture plate which he said he had made from Dr Markwright's specimen. Dr Prince said certainly and started to look through rows of glass discs which were kept on a rack in a cupboard.

As he went on he grew flurried and puzzled and I grew more certain of myself. In the end and after nearly an hour's bewildered search he had to admit that the plate had disappeared. I think he was a bit irritated when I said that of course it had.

Thereafter the puzzle began practically to solve itself. The report from my bacteriologist friend told me, just as I expected, that the ointment I had sent him was, as he put it, "highly contaminated with tetanus spores."

The method, at least, was now clear. The murderer had taken proved tetanus spores from a culture plate and mixed them into the ointment in the cupboard in Dr Markwright's room, and since such a culture plate was missing from Dr Prince's laboratory, it was fairly certainly from that one.

It was nearly the perfect murder. So nearly that everyone except me was satisfied.

What could be more natural? A wound which was entirely accidental. Tetanus setting in—no one could possibly have foreseen that. Death by a disease which is fatal in 90 percent of cases. Yet Mrs Markwright was murdered as surely as Abel.

Why? That was what gave me the answer to the whole thing. Why should anyone want to murder that good, friendly old housewife who never said an unkind word?

The answer was, of course, that no one did. The contaminated ointment had not been intended for her at all, but for her husband. And if for her husband it would not be unreasonable to assume that the same husband had not introduced the tetanus spores.

Then who? You will have guessed. Dr Gudge was arrested as soon as I had been up to the Yard and a warrant had been issued.

It was soon plain to them all. He was a man of infinite patience. Having decided on an almost undiscoverable method, he had bided his time. He had not engineered the little girl's death, but it had been highly convenient to him.

Once Dr Prince had isolated the tetanus bacillus from the specimen it was not difficult for him, during one of his many visits to Prince's laboratory, to pocket the plate.

Then to mix the germs into the ointment gave him no trouble at all and afterwards all he had to do was to wait for Dr Markwright to cut his finger or something and the job would be done for him.

Motive? There was plenty, as I had guessed. The practice to himself and perhaps even more potent, his life-long jealousy of Markwright's popularity.

But Gudge was not a sane man, as he showed us all later when he decided not only to make a confession, but a boastful one, ending up with the fact that he was still using the culture plate he had stolen from Dr Prince as an ash-tray. In spite of the ingenuity of it, it wasn't really a difficult case to solve once I had made my initial guess.

What led me to that? Just what I was telling you. When you're a local policeman you get to know things.

And people—you know people better than any of your psychiatrists and such. I knew Gudge. Cunning as a wagonload of monkeys. Infinitely patient. And a killer, if I ever saw one.

He nearly got away with that perfect murder they all talk about. Only he happened to murder the wrong person.

➤➤◄◄ Beef and the Spider

"That's him," said Sergeant Beef un-grammatically. "That's the murderer. The one getting out of that car. You'd never have thought it of him, would you?"

I would not and I said so with some force to my old friend Beef.

"Well, he is," said Beef aggressively. "I haven't been working on this case for nothing. He done . . . did it, I tell you, as sure as eggs is eggs."

"But can you prove it?" I asked.

"Not yet. But I will do. I just need one more little piece of evidence and we'll hang him."

"Who is he?" I asked.

"Come in here, and I'll tell," Beef replied, steering me through a door into a saloon bar which was deserted at that early hour. He ordered two pints of beer, and we sat down.

"The man I pointed out to you is Sir Oswald

65

Pitcairn, Bart. He owns the big brick works here. Most of the land round here belongs to him too." Beef paused to get one of the little dramatic effects which he loved. "He murdered his brother," he said at last.

I knew that a few months ago Sir William Pitcairn, the brother in question, had disappeared one morning on his way to his office at the brick works just down the road. His body was found in the canal by a bargee some thirty miles from here.

His head had been smashed in, and it had seemed clearly a case of murder. His death, moreover, had occurred only a fortnight after he had inherited the title and a large sum of money from his uncle.

"The obvious suspect was his brother, the man I pointed out to you just now, Sir Oswald Pitcairn. He was a rather shady solicitor, always short of money, and, had his brother not met his end providentially at that moment, I believe that Oswald would have been prosecuted for embezzling his clients' money. But on his brother's death he inherited the title and the money went with it."

"Still, that seems. . ."

"Wait a minute," commanded Beef, raising one of his great red hands. "There's more to it than that. Oswald Pitcairn's engraved wrist-watch was found on the canal bank near where the body had been pushed into the water. An open-and-shut case, everyone thought, until we began our investigation. Then we came up against a brick wall, and unless I get this little bit of extra evidence there won't be a hope of bringing Oswald to justice."

"How's that?" I asked obligingly.

"Well, this William Pitcairn had been out to a club dinner the night before his body was found battered to death.

"His wife, who is a bit of an invalid, heard him drive his car into the garage about one o'clock in the morning. She had been half asleep, but she heard him come in as usual.

"Some time later he came to her room and said goodnight and in the morning he brought her tea as he always did, asked her if she wanted anything, and then, she heard him leave the house to go to his office.

"That was nine o'clock. She knew because the nine o'clock news was just beginning. He always left about then so that he could walk to his office and be there by nine-thirty.

"He never arrived at his office. When it was discovered he was missing, a search was made but it wasn't until the late afternoon that his body was found, and that was only by a lucky chance. It might have lain in the water there for a week without being seen. It was a deserted part of the canal.

"Now what killed the case against the brother was that that very morning Oswald Pitcairn had one of his rare cases in court. He was there first thing, and never left except for lunch, which he had with the town clerk and another solicitor. This was vouched for by a dozen people, including the chief constable. The first case was called at nine-twenty, and Oswald Pitcairn was in the courtroom then. It was impossible for him, therefore, to have murdered his brother that morning, driven some 30 miles each way, and got back, all between nine o'clock when William left home and nine-twenty when Oswald was seen in court.

"There was no possibility of William's wife mistaking the time because of the wireless news; and, besides, that was her husband's normal time of going to work, and there was no reason why he should have varied it that morning.

"Oswald Pitcairn explained away his wristwatch being found by the canal by saying the silver strap was almost broken, and his brother was going to repair it for him. This was quite plausible as William Pitcairn's hobby was doing such odd mechanical jobs, and the strap was found to be faulty. Nothing further has so far come to light."

Beef paused. I took advantage of this to fetch two more pints and light a cigarette. He was already puffing away at his huge pipe.

"But I know the truth," he boasted. "And do you know what first put me on to the solution? A spider. Ever seen a spider's web being shaken by a spider?" Beef asked.

I nodded.

"Do you know why spiders do it? I'll tell you. It's only the male that does it. He's smaller than the female and he wants to tell her that it's he coming into the web and to be careful not to make a meal of him. They've no other sense to recognise each other. Do you see now, why the spider gave me the key to the mystery?"

"Not yet, I'm afraid," I answered.

"As I see it, it happened like this," Beef continued. "Oswald Pitcairn is desperate for money and knows he's facing a long term of imprisonment for embezzlement if he can't get it. So he decides to murder his brother.

"He has always been jealous of William and he needs the money badly. He chooses the eve of a day on which he himself is going to be in court and phones his brother saying he must see him urgently that evening. He probably knew his brother was dining out and fixes the appointment for after dinner.

"They meet, and Oswald, on some pretext, gets his brother to drive out of the town. Oswald then kills his brother, puts the body in the back of the car and drives off, to the canal bank, where he's already reconnoitered a deserted spot.

"He takes his brother's keys and then dumps the body in the water. He has to do this, so that the temperature of the water will conceal the actual time of death. He then drives to his brother's house.

"He has often stayed there, and he's made a study of his brother's habits, which was fairly easy, because William was notoriously methodical.

"Following his brother's exact routine and using his keys, he puts the car away and enters the house. His sister-in-law, being an invalid, is so used to following the usual nightly movements of her husband by the various sounds, that no suspicion crosses her mind that it is not William who opens her door and says, 'Goodnight, darling.' The voice and build of the two brothers bore a strong family likeness.

"Next morning, Oswald gets up at his brother's usual hour, bathes and shaves exactly as he has watched his brother do, makes a pot of tea and, clothed in his brother's dressing-gown, he enters his sister-in-law's bedroom, having first switched off the electricity at the main in case she turns on her reading lamp.

"He knows the blinds will still be drawn on a winter morning—it was January—and that his sister-in-law is always half asleep at that time anyhow. He puts down the cup and only asks her if she wants anything when his back is turned and he is on the way out of the room. He then leaves the house, having looked to see that nobody is about.

"Living alone he is not missed at his own flat, but 'just in case' he probably ruffled his bed the night before and left the remains of a breakfast. Then all he has to do is to appear in court and stay in full view of witnesses whom everyone would trust until his brother's body is found.

"His sister-in-law, like the spider, is convinced that the sounds she heard were made by her husband. She told the police that her husband returned the night before in his car and left for his office as usual at nine by her wireless, and of course nobody, herself included, ever doubted the fact. Now you see why I called Sir Oswald Pitcairn a murderer. But I'd never have tumbled to it if it wasn't for that spider."

"A very good story, Beef," I said. "You may even be right, but you must admit it's only theory. There isn't one fact to prove it."

"No, there isn't," Beef replied thoughtfully. "But I tell you what. I'm going to see Sir William's widow again this afternoon. I haven't lost hope of getting that little piece of evidence I need. You can come with me, if you like," he added handsomely.

At four o'clock that afternoon we were shown into the drawing-room of a small house to which Lady Pitcairn had retired after her husband's death. She was sitting in her wheelchair.

"I hate to re-open a painful subject, Lady

Pitcairn," Beef said. "But I've often wondered whether you've ever had any fresh idea of what really happened to your husband. Did you ever think of anything curious that occurred either the day before he died or the morning of his death? Anything unusual? Perhaps some small thing has come to you since?"

"Well, Sergeant," Lady Pitcairn said. "It's funny you should ask that. One small point has rather worried me. I have never mentioned it to the police because the shock of my husband's death drove it clean out of my mind at first and since then it hasn't seemed important."

"What was it?" Beef asked eagerly.

"Such a small thing. You remember my husband always brought me a cup of tea every morning. Well, on the day of his murder, he brought it as usual, but it wasn't until after I heard him slam the front door that I took a sip and found he had put sugar in.

"That really was extraordinary of him. You see, neither my husband nor I ever took sugar in our tea. Now, Oswald always did. But there, I often wonder whether there was something on my husband's mind that morning which made him thoughtless. Perhaps he wasn't himself."

⇥⯈⬤⬤⯇ Summons to Death

"I never got the credit in that case," said Sergeant Beef regretfully. He was talking about a murder mystery of many years ago when he had been a young constable. "That was because they never gave me a chance to collect the evidence."

He sucked the ends of his ginger moustache when he had dipped them into his pint pot and swallowed gratefully. Then he told his story.

The man murdered was an amiable old solicitor who had not an enemy in the world. Kibble, his name was, and he practised in the little country town of Pyebridge. He was trusted and liked and had a pretty good business. His offices were large and rather grand for that time and place, big lofty rooms in one of the bank buildings. Beef visited him there more than once and thought how enterprising Kibble was to have two or three clerks and a girl sitting at the telephone switchboard and a waiting-room with leather armchairs, all for Pyebridge. But Kibble's business probably justified it.

He was murdered on the same day as Pyebridge lost its most important citizen—Simeon Denes, who lived out at Patchfield, a large house nearly a mile from the town.

Old Denes was rich and a bit eccentric. He had two sons, and that was what made the mystery over Kibble's death.

Denes had decided to cut both his sons out of his will and leave all his money to charity. His reason for this was never known, or what had transpired between him and the two of them in the few days before his death, but from the police point of view it did not matter greatly.

The important thing was that *both* had been beneficiaries and *both* were to be cut out, so that they had an equal interest in seeing that the new will should never be signed.

On the morning of the day on which Kibble was murdered, old Mr Denes sent for him and gave him the details of what he wanted him to do. There was no mystery about this—the clerks in Kibble's office were able to give evidence of the terms of the new will.

It was a rush job, Beef explained, because Denes knew he hadn't long to live and was determined, as only an obstinate and angry man could be, that his sons should not inherit his money. Kibble started drafting it that very afternoon and he managed to finish it before the clerks went home.

Late in the afternoon one of the sons of old Denes came in to see Kibble. He wanted to know whether his father had made any alterations in his will. This was Gerald Denes, the younger son, a well-fed, hard-drinking man who was popular in the town and played cricket for the local team. Kibble told him, of course, that he could not discuss a client's business, and there was a bit of an argument between them.

Kibble stayed late at his office. That was never fully explained, but perhaps no explanation was necessary. His work had probably been upset by his suddenly having to concentrate on drafting the will. He packed up and went out into the High Street at about eight o'clock, when Beef was just going on duty.

"Evening, Constable," he said, for as Beef

told me long afterwards, Kibble always found time to pass the time of day.

"Evening, sir. You're late tonight."

"Yes, and I haven't finished yet. I've got to walk out to Patchfield to see old Mr Denes. His son has just phoned to say he's dying."

Kibble was battered to death on his way out to Patchfield that evening. The will which he had drawn up was not found on his body and no version of it was ever signed, for in the small hours of the morning, old Denes died a peaceful and perfectly natural death.

Beef was young and inexperienced, but he saw that he was right in the middle of an interesting mystery. It was clear to everyone that one of the two sons had murdered Kibble.

Beef made his report, honourably not omitting his conversation with Kibble or the latter's mention of a phone call. This he believed to be the key to the whole thing. If he could find out who had telephoned Kibble he would have a pretty good idea of who had murdered him, or who had knowingly assisted the murderer.

The information given in the call was in any case false. Old Denes had shown signs of recovery in the early part of the evening and the doctor's hopes had risen.

Not waiting for the CID to start investigations Beef called at the local telephone exchange and interviewed Miss Riggs, the young lady who had been in sole charge that evening.

Only one call had been made to Mr Kibble's number after six o'clock that evening. It had come from Pyebridge 909—Mr Oliver Denes's number.

Beef persuaded the CID officer investigating to allow him to be present when Oliver was interviewed.

It was soon apparent that his alibi was un-breakable. Not only did his wife and young son confirm that he had not left the house that evening but the local auctioneer, a most solid and reliable person, had come to dinner and been with Oliver from seven o'clock until near-ly ten. Since Kibble's body had been found at half-past ten and he had then been dead for about two hours, Oliver could not have com-mitted the act of violence which had killed him.

Beef said that he felt excited when the CID man asked Oliver whether he had made any telephone calls that night.

"Telephone calls? Yes, I phoned poor old

Kibble. I'd heard some foolish rumour about my father changing his will and I wanted to know if there was any truth in it."

"You did not tell him your father was dying?"

Oliver looked as though he was trying to be patient with a fool.

"How could I tell him that?" he asked. "I had no idea how my father was. Hadn't seen him since the day before."

Gerald's movements were more difficult to trace, for no one had seen him between the time he left Kibble at half-past five and a brief appearance of his at the Knifegrinders' Arms at a quarter-past eight.

He accounted for this hiatus in the traditional way—he had been to the pictures. Then again, he was known to have been at the Eagle at nine, but opinions differed as to how long he had been there when the nine o'clock news started. He had announced at the Knifegrinders that he was going to the Eagle, and at the Eagle that he had just come from the Knifegrinders.

"I suppose he could have done it," said the CID man to Beef. "He had a car and could have nipped out to Patchfield, murdered Kibble and come back all between his leaving one pub and reaching the other. People don't notice times exactly.

"But if he did, what about the phone call? If he didn't make it he must have known about it, or how could he tell that Kibble would be taking that road at that time?"

"Funny, isn't it?" said Beef in his most annoying way.

"There's only one way in which it can have happened," said the CID man. "The two brothers were in it together. Carefully planned job. Synchronised watches. Clever idea. Close collusion between the two. Don't you agree, young Beef?"

When he reached this point in his story Beef, no longer "young" Beef, scratched his head.

"I didn't agree," he said. "You see, I liked and trusted Oliver. Good darts-player. I didn't believe he'd had anything to do with it. On the other hand Kibble had been summoned to his death by telephone and the one call to his office had come from Oliver's house.

"I puzzled over it for a long time. Then all of a sudden it came to me and I went and gave the case in a nutshell to the CID man. As I told you, he collected the evidence and took the credit. Haven't you tumbled to it yet?"

I shook my head.

"That phone call!" said Beef. "It was his death summons, wasn't it? Whoever made that phone call was the murderer, as I saw it, anyway. Only one call had come from outside.

"But what about *inside*? I told you there was a switchboard, didn't I? And I told you this happened many years ago—before the automatic exchanges.

"What Gerald done—did—was to stay somewhere in those offices from the time he had his interview with Kibble till the time Kibble received the call. Then, when he'd left it as late as he dared, he rang through to Kibble's office from the main switchboard and told him his father wanted him urgently.

"Kibble would never have known, for the ring on an extension in those days was the same whether it came from the outside or inside. Whether Gerald left the building before or after Kibble I never knew. But he was out at Patchfield ready to do him in.

"Simple, wasn't it? All right. What's yours?"

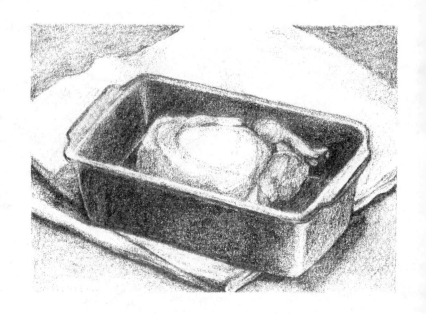

➤➤▮◄◄ The Chicken and the Egg

Which came first—the chicken or the egg? asked Sergeant Beef rhetorically. That's what I had to decide (he went on) when I was investigating the death of Mr Rumple. Which was cause and which was effect. In one case it would mean what it appeared to be—a suicide. In the other, a particularly nasty murder.

Particularly nasty because you couldn't have found a more harmless old bird than little Freddy Rumple.

I was still in the force then, a young constable with a country beat. I knew old Mr Rumple well: a plump man, a widower, who cared for his neighbours and liked children and animals.

He lived simply in spite of his wealth. He had an old house right in the main street and a housekeeper, a Mrs White, and one young woman to help her whom everyone called Daffy.

He had two particular friends, neither of them very young and since he had no near relatives he had made a will, or so everyone said, by which these two would be his heirs after provision had been made for Mrs White and Daffy. One of the friends was Mervyn Plaxton, the schoolmaster, and the other was Farrell Winch, a retired insurance man.

This is what happened. I was on duty in the village square at noon on a bright summer day when one of the schoolchildren came dashing up to me and said —"Come quick, Mr Beef. It's old Mr Rumple!"

There was a crowd gathered already, which was rare in a village like ours, and I had to tell them to stand back there and push my way to the centre. And there was all that remained of poor old Rumple, dead, of course, with his skull smashed.

At the back of old Mr Rumple's house was one of those big warehouses or granaries which you find in Kent and Sussex, built on three floors and having long twelve-paned windows. This one had sliding doors on both its upper floors, and the old gantry was still there from the time when they hauled up the sacks of grain. Old Rumple had had the upper floor turned into a workshop where he used to amuse himself making models of all sorts at a big bench.

On a day like this he would keep the sliding doors open, and when I looked up they were open still.

I saw Farrell Winch in the crowd.

"Dreadful thing," he said. "Dreadful. I saw it all. I was coming up the lane when I heard a sort of shout from the upper storey of the granary. Nothing articulate, you understand, just a throaty cry. I looked up, and there was Rumple standing in the wide open space from which the sliding doors had been pushed back. He looked like a man possessed."

"What do you mean by that?" I asked.

"His eyes were staring and sort of glazed, and he was swaying backward and forward over a sheer drop of thirty feet," he said. "I somehow knew that he was going to fall."

"How?"

"I don't know. I was sure of it. I tried to make him pull himself together. 'Rumple!' I shouted. 'Rumple!' and I don't know what else. Then suddenly he pitched forward, as though impelled by something stronger than himself."

I did not much like all this, but there was no doubt at all that Winch had shouted to the dead man before his fall. Several witnesses confirmed it.

Winch had kept his wits about him. Alone of the crowd who stood round the dead body of Mr Rumple in the first moments after his fall, he had thought of looking upstairs in the workshop to see whether anyone had been with him up there. He raced upstairs and maintained that it would have been difficult for anyone to escape from the second storey before he reached it. It was empty, he said.

I set about a routine investigation, and found the first of some curious circumstances. Mervyn Plaxton, the other beneficiary of Rumple's estate, kept his car in a garage made from the old stables under the granary, and at the time of the tragedy, he said, he had been tinkering with the engine. He too had heard Winch's warning shout and the thud of his friend's body on the road beneath and had run out with the rest of the people I had found there.

Then there were Mrs White and Daffy. The former asked rather truculently where I thought she was at that time in the morning. In her kitchen, of course, preparing lunch. Did I think that an Aylesbury duckling would cook itself? As for Daffy, she had been upstairs, she said vaguely, and when I pressed her for a more detailed account of her movements than that she burst into tears.

Finally, she explained that she had always thought the world of Mr Rumple and it had come as a terrible shock to her. She had run out like everyone else to see what had happened and had been one of the first to see the ugly remains of her employer.

I soon became dissatisfied with the idea of a long-premeditated suicide and believed that if Rumple had killed himself it was the result of something he had seen or heard during the hour before his death. He had been over to the house at 11 o'clock to drink, as was his custom, a cup of coffee with Mrs White. He had been affable, even jocular, and had told her happily about the little model coach he was making.

What, I wondered, had gone on in that workshop that morning? Who had been with poor Rumple there, and what had passed to send him reeling to the open doorway? What had caused that long pause on the brink?

I had to resolve these questions and it began to seem that there was something almost supernatural about the case. If someone had been pushing Rumple, Winch must certainly have seen signs of it, even if this person had succeeded in keeping out of sight. And surely no grip on him could have been so steely and sure that he did not even wriggle or struggle against it? Some mechanism perhaps? But there would surely have been signs of that. Some hidden catapult action? But in that case there would have been no pause. I began to return to supposition of suicide.

Then, as I say, I began to ask myself which came first, the chicken or the egg? Which was cause and which effect? And above all, in what order had things happened?

It came to me suddenly. I hurried out of my cottage where I had been sitting smoking a pipe over it. I raced up the staircase of the granary and began making a real examination of the woodwork round the sliding doors. Then— it was one of the most foolhardy things I ever did as a young policeman—I went and arrested Farrell Winch for the murder of Frederick Rumple.

You ought to have seen the Inspector's face

when I told him what I'd done! He swore I'd be out of the police force in no time. A village constable to make an arrest on his own account before the CID had even been informed? But it was all right in the end, you know, because I had not made any mistake and Winch was hanged.

What made me certain? I kept thinking about what he had told me till I started changing the order of events in my own mind. No one knew which had come first, Winch's shout or Rumple's appearance at the double doors. Suppose the shout had caused the appearance instead of the other way about.

Rumple, working away at his bench, hears his old friend call his name outside. He downs his tools and rushes across to the open sliding doors. Suppose that Winch intended him to do just that and had prepared for it. All that was needed was a trip wire a foot above the floor and a couple of feet behind the doors. Too easy.

Poor old Rumple hears Winch, rushes across, and in a moment has crashed to his death, while Winch has a cast-iron alibi. All he has to do is to rush upstairs and remove his wire before anyone else arrives. It was the marks left by this which confirmed my belief.

So there it was—effect before the cause, you might say.

➹➻ On the Spot

For months now the idea had been festering in Detective Inspector Simler's mind. He was, like all good detectives, an imaginative man, and once such a project as this appealed to him he could not help thinking it out in every detail, picturing all the possibilites. The truth of it was he was a little tired of detection; he wanted actually to commit a crime.

It was his business to watch the antics of criminals and to take advantage of the blunders they made. He recognised that they always made blunders, and generally very obvious ones. But with his unique experience, he felt, he could carry it through without the smallest mistake. And it would be easier for him, he reflected. As one of the most important men at the Yard, he might even be entrusted with the investigation of his own crime, a unique experience.

After a while the chance suddenly presented itself, as chances will. It was Goring, that narrow-eyed man, one of his most alert subordinates, who opened Inspector Simler's eyes to certain possibilites, and it was done in a casual way during a conversation they had at tea-time one day. Goring was on a job at the Palace and Parliament Bank, Boyle Street, in the City. There had been certain unanswered questions which had necessitated his presence there for a few days.

"Of course," he said, "it's none of my business, and nothing whatever to do with the work I'm on, but I can't help thinking there are some dam' fools in the world."

"What makes you say that—" asked Inspector Simler quickly. "Dam' fools" were rather in his line at the moment.

"That firm, Pursley, Pettleton and Pursley, get their whole staff's wages in cash every week. Must be a big sum."

"Well—"

"Well—Damn it, Simler, they send a couple of clerks for it on Fridays. Two quite youngish chaps take it off in a taxi down to Silvertown. Isn't that taking a chance—"

Inspector Simler smiled lightly. "Don't you be an alarmist, Goring," he said. "Why, you'd have me believe it's unsafe to send the office boy round to cash my own cheques next!"

Goring shrugged and the conversation was closed, but Inspector Simler had seen his chance. A big sum in notes travelling down to the East End in a taxi. It was a gift. His sudden craving to bring off a successful crime came to a head. He decided to go into the matter.

First, he inspected the route which a taxi-driver would take and found it passed through a certain sleepy street between the precipitous walls of two factories. There was hardly a door in the street, and when he looked down it he saw only two women, a cat, and an old man taking advantage of its solitude to sleep beside his sack. It was reasonable to infer that this was the loneliest spot on the route.

Next, he ran through a number of official files and found the name he wanted. "Critch, William Herbert." A glance through this man's past career and his present calling satisfied Inspector Simler that his memory of him had not deceived him. William Critch was a criminal with two longish sentences already served.

He was at present working under another name as a taxi-driver, but, as Inspector Simler had good reason to believe from his investigation of a recent case, Critch was only too ready to "take a hand" as the expression went, in any little matter that might turn up.

Very slowly, very carefully, Inspector Simler went about his preparations. He did not even go straight to Critch, but took to frequenting a place at which yet another gentleman of doubtful character and one acquainted with the taximan was to be found. It took him just five months to get into his confidence, and thus achieve an introduction to Critch as "a gentleman in his line."

"It would be money for jam," he observed one night to Mr Critch over a friendly glass of bitter—"money for jam. You would get hired by the two clerks, I'd be waiting in Stone Street, which, as I told you, will be lonely as heaven. Then you'll have engine trouble. I'll hold you up—all three of you—and the cash is ours."

Mr Critch considered for a moment. "That's all very well," he said, "but how am I to get hired by those two— you say they come out at eleven o'clock. Well, but who's to say it'll be my taxi they shout for—"

"It may not be. Probably won't. But what's that matter—we can afford to waste time over this. One week you're bound to time your passing to the second they come out, and get engaged. Then we've got them. Of course, as soon as I've cleared out you'll go with them to the nearest police-station, which is round the corner in Mary Street, and join with them in giving a report. You see, you're safe enough. Who in hell is to suspect you—hired by chance—" Inspector Simler leaned across the table. "That's the way detectives think. They'll know you were hailed in Boyle Street—you are just the first taxi passing. They won't think of identifying you with the affair."

Critch looked at him impressed. "By George!" he said. "You seem to know something about it!"

"Yes," said Simler quietly. "I do."

For eleven weeks Critch drove his taxi past the Palace and Parliament Bank in Boyle Street unsuccessfully. Each time he was a little too early or a little too late, and had to come down to Stone Street and report to Simler, who had waited in vain. The detective, however, was in no hurry. He had seen how foolish haste had often been the ruin of a sound criminal device, and was prepared to wait even though, at times, it was difficult for him to arrange his movements so as to allow him to be on hand. Critch saw the strength of patience too. So long as he was engaged as a chance taxi, passing at the moment, he could hardly be suspected of complicity.

On the twelfth Friday, however, Inspector Simler found that he was not the only lounger among the orange peel and dust of Stone Street. Two men stood in the pale sunlight across the road, apparently indifferent to him and everybody else. "A nuisance," thought Inspector Simler. "If it happens this very week I shall have to postpone."

He lit a cigarette and the minutes ticked by, until he saw, gingerly picking its way among the rubbish at the head of the street, a strange green taxi and knew that Critch had missed his birds again. But had he? Could it be that he had changed his taxi? It was evident that this one was going to pull up.

Accustomed to keeping his head in every circumstance, and taking in every aspect of the situation at the same time, Inspector Simler saw, from the corner of his eye, a sudden tenseness in the two loungers across the road.

In that moment he realized the almost sublime coincidence that had come about. Here, under his very eyes, was a poor attempt at his own game. To the criminal mind such a chance as that taxi full of wage money was not to be missed. And criminal minds think alike. There are not two ways of bringing off a successful robbery, and the gentlemen opposite had hit on the same way as he. In a second he was back in his official capacity.

As the taxi came to a stop beside the two men he could see the frightened, realizing faces of the clerks inside it, and then a quick movement from the men on the curb. Like the shriek of a frightened marsh bird his shrill whistle pierced the peace of Stone Street while he stepped across with the levelled revolver he had brought for his own purposes.

Within five minutes the two men and the taxi-driver were under arrest. The latter protested vigorously.

"What's it to do with me—" he said. "I was just going by, and got hired, like anybody else might have been."

Even the sergeant who had arrested him said to Inspector Simler: "Really, sir, he doesn't seem connected with the case. He could only have been engaged by chance."

But Inspector Simler, with a confidence that the other policemen found it hard to understand, coldly replied that he knew what he was about. Nobody, in the stress of the affair, had noticed a second taxi come down the street being driven by Mr. William Critch, which moved on at a hurried signal from Inspector Simler.

The trial was chiefly memorable for the confession of the taxi-driver, who had admitted, under pressure, that he was associated with the two men and had passed by on the chance of being engaged. It was memorable, too, for the judge's congratulation of Simler.

None of the reporters missed Inspector Simler's generous disavowal: "It was due to the smartness of Inspector Goring," he said modestly. "It was Inspector Goring who first remarked on the method with wages of Messrs Pursley, Pettleton and Pursley."

It was graciously done, but of course everyone saw that the credit was Simler's.

"You are being promoted," said his Chief a few days later, "for your smart work in anticipating that attempted robbery. It says much for you that you were actually on the spot. You have, let me tell you, Simler, in my opinion, a quite unique understanding of the criminal mind."

"Thank you, sir," said Simler quietly.

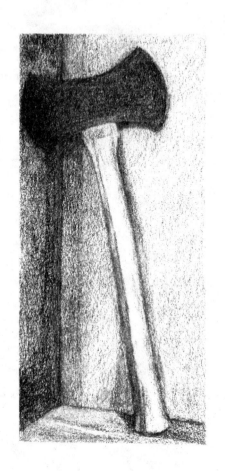

➤➤➤◄◄ Blunt Instrument

Simple? said Sergeant Beef, speaking of a case he had investigated some years before. Yes, it was as simple as Columbus's egg, once you tumbled to it. But it made a lot of them puzzle their heads and try to create complications because it was so straightforward.

The murder itself was like that—the brutal killing of an old woman for the sake of her money. No, I wasn't in charge of the investigation. The CID did that. You might say I acted as an adviser. It was the first case given to young Thackeray who had been a constable under me when he joined the Force. Smart young fellow he was and soon found himself at the Yard. So I gave him what you might call the benefit of my experience.

The murder took place in a quiet village in the Southern counties.

The smaller of the two village shops was kept

by a Mrs Green, an elderly widow who lived alone there and had the reputation for being a bit of a miser. On a rainy night in the autumn the local policeman, Constable Maugham, was going his rounds at about midnight when he noticed that the door of Mrs Green's shop was ajar.

He entered the shop and began to look about him. Then he saw by the end of the counter a very gruesome spectacle. Mrs Green lay in what could only be described, even in the coroner's court afterwards, as a pool of blood.

She was a little woman and Maugham told me afterwards he could scarcely have believed there could be such signs of butchery from one murder. Her skull had been cleft by one big blow from an axe. And lying beside her was the very axe that had been used—a heavy two-handed affair.

Constable Maugham acted correctly and before the people of the village had sat down to breakfast, unconscious of the crime that had been committed, a doctor had examined the body and the CID boys had been sent from the county town.

The hunt, in fact, was on. But who was to be

hunted? It was about as blank as a case could be.

There was the doctor's evidence that Mrs Green had been killed by a single blow of the axe from someone standing in front of her at about six or seven o'clock on the previous evening. "Between five and eight" was the gist of his calculation.

There were no fingerprints. No one had been seen to approach the shop. No strangers had been observed in the village. And nothing, it appeared, had been stolen except cash, of which there was a fairly large sum.

A crime of violence, probably unpremeditated, is the hardest of all mysteries for a man to tackle, and Detective-Inspector Thackeray cursed the luck which had given it to him as his first opportunity. He went about his investigation thoroughly and systematically, though, and long before I came into it he had managed to gather some useful information.

First he had found out a good deal about the village and about events there on the evening of the murder. The last customer to be in the shop was a Miss Winch, who had, she said, popped round for some pepper at about five-thirty. Mrs Green had been quite as usual, complaining of taxation and the weather.

"I shall shut up sharp at six," she had told Miss Winch, "to be in time to hear the news. It's been a quiet day, anyhow."

Miss Winch had seen no one approaching as she left the shop and had met no one on her way home. Mrs Green's nearest neighbours were the Blackeys, an elderly couple whose cottage was about a hundred yards away. They had been home all the evening, but had heard nothing amiss.

"I doubt if we should have," said Mrs Blackey chattily, "for my husband's hearing gets worse every day and I was out in the kitchen most of the time with the wireless on. The only person we saw that evening was Jim Cassidy. He passed our gate about seven o'clock when I let the cat out. Yes, up the road towards Mrs Green's. He's a good-for-nothing, of course, but I don't think he would have done *that*."

Thackeray was not so sure. The amiable bad hat, the lazy, drink-loving type for whom everyone is sorry, is no less capable of murder because he has been in fairly harmless trouble all his life. And Cassidy was the only man known to have been near the shop at the prescribed time.

There were two men in the village that evening, however, who had come from elsewhere. There was Tom Buttery, an itinerant knife-grinder who used to come round once or twice a year with his barrow. Most of the housewives knew him and he was generally supposed to be a bit simple, though he was no fool when it came to poaching, or even, it was said, chicken-stealing. Then there was a man called Mothbury, who had arrived at the Woolpack Inn on a bicycle just before six o'clock and was the first to enter the bar when it opened.

"A big unhealthy-looking chap," said the landlord. "He started with whisky and then went on to beer. It's usually the other way about and I couldn't help thinking his money was running out. He left here just after seven. No, not drunk, but with a skinful. Inclined to be argumentative, I thought. I've never seen him before or since."

None of these could rightly be called suspects, though Tom Buttery had done time in his day, because there was nothing to connect them with the crime.

There was one other man, though, who at first

seemed a possibility because he knew a good deal about the murdered woman. This was Ben Willard, who had worked for her for some years, driving the van, helping in the shop, even doing a bit in her garden.

He had reached his home at five o'clock that evening and found that his wife had her sister there. He had remained with the two women, who vouched for his presence, till about eight o'clock, when he went down to the Woolpack, arriving at about eight-fifteen and remaining till closing time.

"No, nothing unusual about him," the landlord said. "Never has much to say for himself, and that night was no exception."

Then Thackeray went into the whole question of the axe. It had certainly been used for the murder as examination of the stains and certain minute portions of fibrous matter on it revealed, and it had certainly belonged to Mrs Green. Thackeray was even able to trace her purchase of it a couple of months earlier at a shop in the market town to which she had gone in the van with Ben Willard.

Here, it seemed, Thackeray had his first piece of luck, for the shopkeeper was most informative.

"I remember it well," he said. "Mrs Green had been a customer of ours for some years, and since we have a wholesale business, too, insisted on buying things at wholesale prices. Her man Willard came into the shop with her that day, since it was for his use that she purchased the axe. I think she would have been content with a smaller and less expensive tool, but Willard explained that it would be useless, and eventually she allowed him his choice."

Ben Willard, questioned, appeared to answer candidly. He had asked Mrs Green to buy a large axe of this kind as she wanted him to cut down two fair-sized trees that winter. No, it had not occurred to him that it could be used as a weapon, in fact he had complained to Mrs Green that it wasn't sharp enough to cut anything much. It was kept in a shed at the back of the house, and he had seen it there that morning when he went for the coal. The shed had been locked when he went home on the evening of the murder, and was still locked when he came the next morning, but both he and Mrs Green had keys. That was all he knew.

All Thackeray knew, too, when he rang me up

and asked me if I would like to come down and look round. All he could tell me when I arrived. What's more, all I knew when I told him who was the murderer. In stating the facts as I have stated them to you, he had given me the one clue, the simple, unavoidable clue to the whole riddle.

Of course, afterwards he had to do a lot of spade work to prove his case. Identifying one of the Treasury notes found in the guilty man's possession. Discovering traces of bloodstains clumsily cleaned from his coat. But it was what I saw, plain as a pikestaff, which identified the murderer.

You haven't seen it? Well, ask yourself how the axe got into the shop.

Ben had left it locked in the shed and the lock was intact next morning. Unless he had come and done it himself the old lady must have brought it out. So since his alibi was cast iron I knew that she must have provided the murderer with his weapon.

You still haven't got it? No, nor had Thackeray till I had pointed out that the only man to whom she would have handed that axe was one who was going to sharpen it for her. A knife-grinder, in fact.

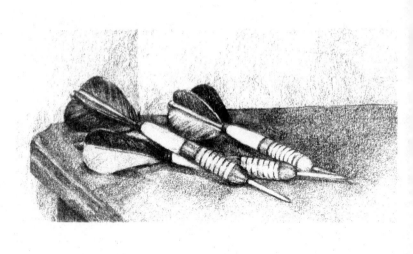

⇥■◀ I, Said the Sparrow

"Are you a toxophilite?" asked young Thackeray. "No, Church of England," said Sergeant Beef quickly as he bisected a large pickled onion.

The CID man sighed.

"I mean, are you any good with a bow and arrow?"

"You trying to be funny?" asked Sergeant Beef. "It's not that long since I retired from the Force."

Thackeray, who had once served as a constable under Beef, knew him well enough to show no impatience. "I asked because I'm investigating this murder out at Tryfford. You must have read about it. Man shot dead with an arrow."

"Let's hear the details," said Sergeant Beef, unable to keep the eager gleam from his eyes.

Thackeray had got what he wanted.

113

"Certainly. Ledwick Jayne was the president of Robin Hood Club of Toxophilites which used to meet at his house once a year for their championship competition. A rich man, Jayne, a widower with one son. This son is a keen-looking type, ex-Army captain, alert and athletic, one of the best archers in the club — if you still call them archers.

"Jayne himself was over 80, a gangling loose-jointed old man. He had a stroke some years ago and it left him not exactly paralysed but stumbling and jerky, with an impediment in his speech and a more or less permanently dropping lower jaw.

"He no longer joined in the archery but never lost his interest in the pastime and made this annual competition a sort of house-party at his great Victorian country house.

"On the night after the finals in which his son Dennis had won the Robin Hood Cup, Ledwick Jayne was standing out on the balcony of his bedroom at ten o'clock before turning in.

"He had said good-night to brother Raymond, with whom he had drunk a last whisky-and-soda in his study and had gone up to his bed.

"His son, who was several hundred yards

away down at the lake, says that he saw him there in the distance, illuminated by his bedroom light behind him. Dennis, the son, thought nothing of it, for his father was a creature of habit.

"All the younger members of the party had gone down to the lake according to a plan made at dinner. It was a very warm night and they decided that it would be fun to go there and perhaps take a boat out. It was near the field in which the competition had been held, and the little pavilion where they kept their bows and arrows was beside it.

"Ledwick's brother tells the rest of the story. He, Raymond Jayne (an accountant who specialises in income-tax claims), had a last whisky after Ledwick had departed. He had to ring for more soda and chatted with Parkins, the manservant, while he drank it.

"Then he went upstairs. His room was next to his brother's, and the window was open. Suddenly he heard the sound of a fall with breaking wood and ran into Ledwick's room to find him lying over a smashed deckchair on his veranda.

"It was not very light out there, and only when he had hauled his brother's body into the room did he see the arrow. It had gone straight through the roof of Ledwick's mouth to his brain. The older man was stone dead."

"Let's hear the rest of the facts," said Beef.

"There aren't many.

"A bow, one of those which had been used by the competitors that day, was found among the bushes across the lawn. The angle of the arrow's entry would be just right if it had been shot from there.

"The suspects are necessarily those of the practised toxophilites who were out there in the grounds at the time of the murder."

"Or those of them who had any motive," put in Beef.

"Well, they all had, more or less, except perhaps a Mr Newnes Drury. You see, they were relatives. The Toxophilite Club was largely a family affair and Ledwick used to ask all those related to him to stay in the house. The rest put up at the village inn a mile or two away and were all in the bar at the time.

"Down by the lake were Raymond's two sons, Keith and Alec, and a girl friend of Keith's called Nancy Maynard. There was also Ledwick's daughter, Grace.

"I say they are all suspects because Ledwick was a very rich man, and his will, which I have examined, divides up his fortune in the way you would expect — large shares to his son and daughter, then slightly smaller equal shares to his brother and nephews.

"Any one of them would receive enough money to start him or her in whatever career chosen and Raymond's share would make the rest of his life comfortable.

"The man without any apparent motive, this Newnes Drury, may possibly have had some understanding with Ledwick's daughter, but I can find no evidence of it. So there you are. Six people under 30, all out on the grounds when Ledwick was shot, mostly having a motive, and all expert archers."

"Fingerprints?" asked Beef.

"Gloves are worn by archers, I believe. They were by this one, anyway. The arrow hadn't a print. The bow had been used that afternoon by Dennis and Keith, and there were good prints of each of them. Nothing else."

"No footprints?"

"Rubbed out."

"What was the distance from the point where

the murderer was believed to stand to Ledwick's position?"

"About twenty yards."

"Was it, though?" said Beef, for the first time showing animation. "Twenty yards? That's interesting."

There was a long silence. Then Thackeray picked up his notes.

"I can tell you what each of the young people claims to have been doing at the time. Of course, they've only got one another as witnesses. Keith and his girl friend had taken the punt and pushed out on the lake. . . ."

"Never mind all that," said Beef brusquely. "Have you got someone down at Tryfford now?"

"Yes. Coles is there."

"Can you phone him?"

"I daresay. What do you want to know?"

Beef sat back in his chair.

"There's several things. I ought really to go down myself. I'm getting old and lazy. Still, you tell your chap to get the manservant to the telephone and I'll do the talking."

Beef thoughtfully poured out a glass of beer while Thackeray did as he was asked.

"We're pretty sure that Parkins never went out that night," he said, with his hand over the receiver. "No other servants lived in the house."

Beef nodded, and when at last the manservant was at the other end asked his questions with great deliberation.

"You remember that night. Did you put the whisky and soda out for Mr Jaynes and Mr Raymond? You did? Well, how much whisky was there and how much soda?"

Thackeray, leaning close, could hear the man's metallic-sounding reply.

"The siphon was nearly full. The whisky decanter about a third full."

"And when Mr Raymond rang? Did you notice?"

"Yes. I took particular notice because I was surprised. The siphon was empty. About half the whisky had gone."

"They like it drowned, did they?"

"No. That struck me as queer at the time. They both liked only a spot of soda."

"Then, when you finally took the tray away?"

"That night, it was. After Mr Raymond had gone up. The decanter was empty and the new siphon about an inch down."

"You stopped there chatting to Mr Raymond?"

"I couldn't help it. He kept questioning me about my family and that. I wanted to get back to my fire."

"Thank you, Parkins. You've been most helpful. Are you a toxophilite, by the way?"

"No, sir. I shouldn't know what to do with a bow and arrows."

"Nor should I," laughed Beef and replaced the receiver.

"Well?" Thackeray sounded impatient.

"Clever," said Beef. "Dead clever. You'll have to work hard to get the evidence together if you mean to hang him. I can tell you the murderer. At least, I'm pretty sure of it. But you'll have to get the proof."

"Go on," said Thackeray.

"Why did Raymond ring for Parkins?" Beef asked. "And insist on keeping him talking for ten minutes or more? There had been a full siphon of soda. It couldn't have all been used. Why did he squirt it away so that he had an excuse for getting Parkins up to the study if he didn't want to create an alibi for himself?"

"He knew when Ledwick would be shot,

then?"

"He knew when Ledwick would die. Let me ask you another question. Do you think that any man with a bow and arrow, any man, mind you, could shoot another through his open mouth at twenty yards range in half darkness?

"If you do you've never played darts. You may be able to get a full once in three darts, but change your length of throw by two feet and you won't get on the board.

"These archers practised on targets, not on deer in Sherwood Forest. There was not one of them who could even have hit a man's head at an unmeasured range. I saw that at once. Ledwick was not shot from the garden. He was poisoned by his very clever brother.

"All Raymond had to do when he administered his poison in the whisky was to let Ledwick go to bed and keep Parkins in a closed room far away from the bell. He knew that he would not be disturbed for he had heard the young people's plans and was aware that Parkins was the only resident servant.

"So when he had kept Parkins long enough he went up and found his brother neatly stretched out dead. He had his arrow ready and thrust it through the roof of his mouth to the brain so that he could 'find' his brother shot from the shrubbery.

"He had already emptied away the rest of the whisky which contained the poison and washed out the decanter with soda-water. He broke the deck-chair with a couple of kicks — a nice touch that.

"His alibi was cast-iron. His brother, standing on the balcony with six skilled archers in the grounds, is shot through his notoriously wide open mouth.

"Who's going to suspect poison? The cause of death could never be doubted for a moment, he thought, a cause with which he could have no connection. But you go and get a post-mortem and see if I'm not right. There's something very convincing about a bow and arrow but really, when you come to think of it. . ."

"Exactly," said Thackeray, "when you come to think of it."

➤❚❰❰ A Piece of Paper

The most unpleasant case I ever had to deal with [said Sergeant Beef], happened in a little town not far out of London, where I was in charge. For sheer villainy I've never know its equal.

It started off quite straightforward. I was called round to a house called Merrywell at eight o'clock in the evening. Mrs Gribley, a comfortable old party whom I knew quite well, had taken an overdose of sleeping tablets and was dead.

She and old Bert Gribley, her husband, were known as a devoted couple — proper Darby and Joan, people said. Both of them were wrapped up in their son Raymond, who was a very promising medical student. They were well off, and it was understood that Mrs Gribley had the money. She was generous, though, particularly with the young Raymond, who had a sports car and a flat in town and only came down at week-ends.

Bert Gribley told a simple but tragic story. He had been up in London all day and had reached his home at seven o'clock. He had found his wife dead in her armchair by the fire, with the half-empty bottle of his sleeping tablets, pre-scribed for him some months ago by the local doctor, beside her.

On the table, in Mrs Gribley's handwriting, was a note which Bert handed to me: "I cannot be separated from my dear ones. I cannot go on. Let no one be blamed for my death, which is of my own seeking. — Clara Gribley."

That, you will admit, was about as clear-cut a suicide note as you can find, so much so that I wondered if there could be any chance of forg-ery. It is not often that a suicide is as explicit as that. I may as well say now that the hand-writing experts confirmed later that it had in-deed been written by Mrs Gribley.

That, you would say, was the end of it. I don't even now know why I was not satisfied, but there were several little things which were not quite usual. First of all, what had she meant by her "dear ones"? I asked Bert Gribley that.

"I don't know," he said, "it puzzles me, too. The only people I know of whom she could call her 'dear ones' are me and Raymond. Of course she lost her parents years ago and her sister died last April, but these were just ordinary family losses. She was not particularly devoted to her sister."

I asked him what state of mind she had been in when he saw her.

"When I left this morning she was perfectly all right. She was always a cheerful woman and today as much as ever."

There was another thing that struck me as not quite as one would expect, that was the fact that some of the sleeping tablets were left in the bottle. Suicides usually like to make very sure.

"I bought a new supply yesterday," said Bert. "I get them twenty at a time. She seems to have taken ten of them."

It must have been some sort of intuition which made me ask if I might take a look round before I left. Bert said that of course I could, and I made a routine search.

The only thing I found which could be of any interest was a slip of paper on the floor with two words on it in Mrs Gribley's writing.

"Deeply regret," I read. I supposed that this was a false start and she had put it aside to write the note she eventually left.

For the next few days I worked hard on the case and found out one or two interesting things. Young Raymond had been in the district that afternoon, for instance. This was nothing out of the way because he had a girl in the town who worked at a hairdresser's and this was her afternoon off.

I asked him whether he had been up to Merrywell and he said no, he had not had time. He had left his girl at about four o'clock and hurried back to London where he had arrived before six.

Then Mrs Gribley's brother came forward to say he had had tea with the dead woman at four o'clock and stayed with her till nearly half-past. She had been cheerful as usual, quite unpreoccupied, he thought, and had eaten a good tea.

He knew of nothing to explain the suicide or her reference to her "dear ones." I checked on his movements very thoroughly and found that he had been back at his home, three miles away, at about five.

Bert Gribley's movements were equally easy to check. He had left London by the 5:35 train with a man called Saunders, whose home was a few yards from his own. They had walked up from the station together and stopped at Saunders' house to hear on the wireless the result of the first race at Newmarket because they had both backed the same horse. As soon as Bert knew that he had not won, he left for his home.

Well, there it all was, and I felt I ought to be satisfied but I still felt uncomfortable. The post-mortem told us nothing.

Then I heard something that made me think. A week earlier Mrs Gribley had sent for a local solicitor called Cowley and asked him to draw up a new will. Her previous one had been made when she was married and had left every-thing to Bert, except for a lump sum to her brother.

She explained now that the two older men would have enough for their needs from their respective businesses and she wished to leave her entire fortune to Raymond. Mr Cowley had almost completed the preparation of this docu-ment and would have been bringing it to her for signature in a day or two, for Mrs Gribley had already passed the draft.

That made it all even more perplexing. I still did not see how it could be anything but suicide, for the note was conclusive enough. But if it were — then this might provide a motive for any one of the three men, since the husband or brother could be preventing the signature of the will and the son might have supposed it was already signed.

I decided to concentrate on that piece of paper which I had found at Merrywell. "Deeply regret" were the only words on it and I kept turning these over in my mind. Surely they were not the beginning of a suicide message? They were too solemn and yet formal for that.

If she were about to regret causing pain she would have said so and started "I am sorry. . ." How could those words have been used? Something pretty serious, certainly. The beginning of a message giving very bad news and since they were in her handwriting, and the experts said the ink was only a few hours old, a message she had received, a message which might account for the change in her from the cheerful woman her brother left at 4:30 and the suicide of two or three hours later.

I reasoned on. The message had come by telephone, then. A telegram read out—quite a usual thing in our district. I checked again and was stumped, for no telegram had been sent to Merrywell that day.

Then suddenly an idea came.

What message could have turned this amiable, elderly woman into a suicide? There were only two possibilities—announcements of the death of either her husband or her son.

If someone had got through to her number and said in an unfamiliar voice that he had a telegram for Gribley and had gone on, "Deeply regret to inform you that your husband (or your son) died at such-and-such a time from such a cause," would not that account for everything?

No. Not quite everything. For whichever had died the other would remain, claiming her love and needing her. It was impossible—or virtually impossible—for them to have died together. So finally the whole thing fell into place.

Bert Gribley knew that his wife was leaving all her money to their son and that he had to act at once if he were to prevent this.

Before catching his train in London that evening he phoned to his home and disguising his voice by holding his nose (an ancient expedient) he dictated a telegram announcing that Raymond had been killed in an accident. He reached his house at about 6:20 or so and not at seven o'clock as he claimed, for at Saunders' home a few yards away he heard a racing result which was broadcast at about 6:16 and immediately left for home.

There he found his wife prostrate with grief, and in half an hour had persuaded her into a suicide pact. What was there left for either of them? he asked. With his new supply of sleeping tablets they could take ten each and go together peacefully. Clara would be with him and Raymond and so would not have to leave her 'dear ones.' They would each write a last note to avoid any possible ambiguity.

The poor woman must have agreed quite promptly, for before seven o'clock they had written their notes and Clara was dead, believing that her husband had swallowed his share.

All Bert had to do then was to destroy his own note and send for the doctor and police and show us how he had found his wife, handing us her quite genuine statement of intention to commit suicide.

I might never have been able to charge him, though I knew that instigation to suicide was murder in itself, but the evidence was all pretty flimsy up to then and a lot of it guesswork.

What helped me was his overconfidence. He was so sure of himself that when he was confronted with the accusation of the telegram, he admitted having sent it. Apparently he thought it had been seen in the telephone booth. He pretended regret for what he called a silly practical joke.

It took me days to get him any farther than that, but in the end he confessed, under the impression that one of two in a suicide pact cannot be charged with murder. Funked it at the last minute, he claimed.

➔➤➤◄◄ Letter of the Law

"A very neat little murder," thought Mr Ziccary as he washed his hands at the kitchen sink. "Remarkably neat for a beginner."

The body of his wife lay six feet deep under the floor of his cellar and the flagstones showed no signs of having been disturbed for a hundred years or more.

"Since they were first laid," thought Mr Ziccary, knowing that the remote and isolated grey house in which he had lived alone with Emily had been built about a century ago.

It was very improbable that anyone would examine the cellar floor or anything else about the place, or even ask him any awkward questions. But if they did he had The Letter.

Typical of Emily. So careless and slapdash, as she had always been during the fifteen years of her marriage to Mr Ziccary. Making silly mistakes and changing her mind. When he

135

received the letter, a year ago now, he saw its possibilities almost at once. It was scrawled in pencil, for instance, and that was an excellent medium for Emily to have chosen, since no expert could say how long ago it had been written. It was dated November 1 quite clearly, with no day of the week before it and no year after it.

"Dear Abel," it ran in her unmistakable spidery hand. "I have left you. I couldn't stand that lonely life so far from people to talk to any longer. A man whom I like and respect has taken me away and I've no doubt you will be glad. If you will send on any of my things address them to Miss Potter to be called for at Victoria Station. Your wife, Emily."

Then, of course, after she had put the letter on the mantelpiece and walked down the lane to wait for her friend, the man had failed to turn up. Again, typical of Emily. Burning her boats too soon. Mr Ziccary found the letter, put it carefully between the pages of a book and went out to find his wife and bring her back.

A year ago. He smiled smugly. Exactly a year ago, for he had been waiting impatiently for the date. November 1 fell on a Tuesday this year and on that evening he invited her down to the cellar and quietly murdered her while her back was turned toward him.

No fuss, no incriminating stains on the furniture. Within an hour she lay under the floor in the grave which he had made ready for her weeks before.

Yes, it had all gone like clockwork. To give her the opportunity for her supposed departure on the Tuesday morning, he had gone down to the village and made himself noticed by one of the shopkeepers. At four o'clock he called on the Whistons, his nearest neighbours, half a mile away and told them that he half believed his wife had left him.

"She has talked rather strangely lately," he said, "and when I arrived home at lunch-time she was not there."

Emily was laying his tea at that moment, but he spoke so convincingly that the Whistons gave him a mixture of reassurance and sympathy.

At five o'clock he returned to Emily.

"Anyone called, dear?" he asked, knowing that in such an unlikely eventuality he would have to postpone the matter, at least for another year.

"No one," she said. "I haven't seen a soul."

"Or been seen by one, I suppose?" he added facetiously.

She shook her head. She never lied, so the coast was clear and the rest of his plan followed automatically.

On Wednesday morning he took The Letter, which he was supposed to have received by now, and showed it to the Whistons.

"Where do you think she has gone?" asked Mrs Whiston.

"Well, the postmark was a London one," he said. "A South-Eastern district. But there—I shan't pry into her life now."

Lastly he took her things, packed them and addressed the two suitcases to Miss Potter at Victoria Station as she had requested when she had meant to leave him a year previously. All was now in order and he could settle down to enjoy the money which she had long ago made over to him.

Yet within a short space of time Abel Ziccary was questioned, arrested, tried, found guilty and hanged by the neck until he was as dead as Emily.

When Emily told him that no one had called that afternoon she was telling the truth so far as she knew, but it did not occur to her to mention that Mr Best, the village postman, had cycled out with a small parcel for her.

Nor did it occur to Abel Ziccary, who carried on a wide correspondence with certain charitable people who answered his many advertisements, to notice that there had been one day on which he had by chance received no letters. That was Wednesday.

But it did occur to Mr Best, a shrewd and kindly soul, that if Mrs Ziccary had left her husband on Tuesday morning, as he said, it was odd that she had opened the door to him on Tuesday afternoon. And if Mr Ziccary had received her letter by post on Wednesday, as he maintained, it was curious that there had been no letters for him during that day.

The police thought so, too.

⇥★◄ A Glass of Sherry

"I could murder that woman," said Mrs Plummery. "I know you could, my dear," said her husband more soberly, then added: "Why don't you?"

Mrs Plummery tried to laugh.

"Whatever do you mean, Gillman?"

Mr Plummery was not laughing when he said:

"Exactly what I say, my dear. It would mean thirty thousand pounds for us, even when all the death duties have been paid. That, after all, is worth consideration."

From that exchange of light conversation began the scheming which led to the sudden death of Miss Alicia Greenleaf, aunt and godmother of Freda Plummery.

It took nearly a month of careful planning. Methods were discussed and dismissed as impracticable, but finally one was settled on and a timetable drawn up. The following Thursday

was chosen because on that day Miss Greenleaf's companion, Mrs Tuckey, would be spend-
ing her customary weekly afternoon and evening
with her family.

Miss Greenleaf lived in a fairly large house
just outside the village. She was a vigorous old
lady who, though now in her seventies, worked
in her garden and organised local activites with
energy and efficiency. She gave her opinion
with great frankness and could be extremely
blunt with those around her: it was this blunt-
ness which had made Freda Plummery exclaim
too emphatically that she could murder her aunt.

At six o'clock on that dark December evening
the Plummerys set out from their house to call
on Miss Greenleaf. In the village they went into
a shop and Freda Plummery said she would
carry her purchase with her "as she was going
straight home." They took care not to be seen
approaching Miss Greenleaf's house, and by a
quarter past six they were sitting with her,
talking amiably.

At half-past six, as they had expected, Miss
Greenleaf offered them a glass of brown sherry,
and Freda was able to introduce a strong sopo-
rific into the old lady's drink while Gillman

Plummery held his aunt-in-law's attention. Before seven she was fast asleep in her chair, little stertorous snorts coming from her half-closed lips.

Gillman and Freda smiled at each other, for their plan was going like clockwork. They gently lifted the old lady and laid her on the kitchen floor with her head on a cushion in the gas-oven.

"Nothing clumsy," said Gillman, "like that case where the old man was murdered in this way. That was discovered because he was bruised."

Then they stuffed up any cracks in the room, turned the gas on and left it with the door unlocked but closed.

Now was their most trying hour, for they were determined not to leave the house till they were sure the old lady was dead.

"We don't want any sort of resurrection," said Gillman grimly.

They washed out her sherry glass and sat down together in the sitting-room. If anyone came, after all, they could pretend to be unaware of what was happening in the kitchen and could keep the caller talking here till there was no chance of revival.

But no one did come. At half-past eight, confident that Miss Greenleaf was dead, they quietly left the house and made their way home. Again they took care to escape observation, and were successful in this.

Now came the final phase of the operation, a piece of seeming bravado which would, they believed, divert all suspicion. Freda Plummery telephoned the local police station.

"Is that the police?" she asked. "Mrs Plummery here. I expect I'm just wasting your time, but my husband thinks I ought just to mention something. It's about my aunt, Miss Greenleaf. She was on the phone to us about an hour ago and said something rather extraordinary."

Freda could hear the policeman chuckle at the other end. Everyone knew the extraordinary things which Miss Greenleaf said.

"She said she was going to kill herself. No, we don't take it very seriously coming from her, but we thought we ought just to mention it."

Freda put down the receiver and sighed.

"That's that," she said.

When the police called next day, two plain-clothes men who started by expressing their sympathy, Gillman and Freda Plummery were quite ready for them. But just as they were leaving, one of them asked Freda, "Where was Miss Greenleaf when she phoned you last night?"

"At home," said Freda promptly.

"You are sure of that, Mrs Plummery?"

"Oh, quite. She said she was at home."

"And you were here?"

"Yes."

What could all this mean?

The telephone exchange was an automatic one—there could be no record of calls.

"I ask because from two o'clock yesterday afternoon Miss Greenleaf's phone was out of order."

Freda did not lose her head.

"Well, she *said* she was at home," was the answer.

It did not seem to satisfy the two policemen, for the next day they called again and questioned Freda for over an hour.

"Nothing to worry about," said Gillman. "So long as you don't get flustered. They may suspect but they can never prove anything if you don't tell them."

But she did tell them in the end. After four or five days of their persistent courteous questioning she admitted that she and her husband had been up at the house that night. Caught out in one lie her resolve slowly gave way and finally she confessed everything.

Freda got off with a life sentence. Gillman is to hang next week.

He is furious with his wife.

"Another time," he says savagely, "I'll see that there's no woman in it."

→⥽⥺← The Scene
of the Crime

"Don't you mind living in a house where such a very horrible murder was committed?" asked Mr Stickles primly.

The old gentleman smiled.

"Not in the least. I'm not sensitive to atmosphere. I was able to get the place very cheaply at the time, you see."

"I can quite understand that," said Mr Stickles.

"You want to see the scene of the crime, do you? It's my bedroom now."

"Yes, I'm by way of being a criminologist, you know. An unsolved case like that always interests me. You know all the facts, of course?"

"I've never taken much interest in them," said the old gentleman.

"Well, it happened in 1948. Old Mr Brenner Firclough lived here quite alone. He was a wealthy man and though not exactly a miser, he was far from generous or extravagant. He collected old silver and had a very fine collection.

"On the morning of October 16 the local woman who came in to clean and cook for him could not get an answer at the back door and on her way round to the front noticed a window open. She called the police and they found Mr Brenner Firclough's body. He had been murdered in bed—his throat cut, probably with an open razor. There was what can only be described as a welter of blood. A great deal of the silver had vanished."

"I heard something of the sort," said the old gentleman. "They have never recovered any of the silver, I believe?"

"Never. It is said to have been melted down — which would have been a shameful piece of vandalism. Some of it was priceless."

"I'll take you upstairs now."

Mr Stickles again apologised for coming to the house and introducing himself. He explained that in following his hobby, the study of crime, he sometimes overstepped the margin of good manners. He had seen the name on the house, Bablock, and, remembering the famous Bablock murder, he had ventured to call.

"Don't apologise," said the old gentleman. "I shall be happy to show you whatever you wish to see. I don't get many callers, you know. I, too, live alone here but I have no collection of old silver to tempt the criminal."

They went upstairs and entered a large room with a bay window. There was a high mahogany bed facing it.

"This, I understand, is where it took place."

"Yes," said Mr Stickles. "I have seen a photograph of this room. The corpse was lying in the middle of the bed. The murderer had approached from this side and made only one stroke with his razor."

"It must have been a razor much like this?" suggested the old gentleman, crossing to the dressing-table and picking up an old-fashioned razor case. "You see, I use a cut-throat, too," he added, smiling.

"Exactly," said Mr Stickles. "Held in the right hand and slashed from left to right with downward pressure."

"And the ruffian was never brought to book," reflected the old gentleman absently. He seemed bored with Mr Stickles now—perhaps anxious to return to his warm fireside.

"No," said Mr Stickles. "But I have a theory."

"Indeed?"

The old gentleman almost yawned.

"Yes, I'm pretty sure it was the nephew."

"What makes you think that?" asked the old gentleman politely.

"Something so obvious that anyone should have thought of it. If the intruder had merely come after the silver why should he have troubled to murder Brenner Firclough? There was no sign of a struggle and it seems likely that the old chap was murdered in his sleep. Why, if the man were a burglar?"

"I'm afraid I never thought of that."

"No. It was someone who had a motive. The theft of the silver in my opinion was a blind. And as the nephew was Brenner Firclough's sole heir he would seem to be the only person with a motive."

"But I seem to remember that the nephew was on the other side of the globe at the time."

Mr Stickles nodded.

"Australia," he said. "Well, he *was* there two days before it happened and forty-eight hours after the murder, booked his passage home on a liner leaving shortly after.

"But you know psychologically we're still blind to the possibilities of air travel. Because two days after the crime the nephew received an airmail letter in Sydney and at once booked his passage. It simply doesn't occur to us that he could himself have flown home, committed the murder and returned to Australia.

"When the possibility is pointed out we recognize it. Till then the man has what amounts to an alibi."

"Very interesting," said the old gentleman. "But what about the silver?"

"I'm coming to that," said Mr Stickles. "If my theory is correct it was probably concealed at the time—that very night, in fact. I have a strong conviction that it is at the bottom of the pond in the garden."

"Good gracious me," said the old gentleman.

"I will not conceal the fact that I am hoping to persuade you to have that pond emptied or dragged. You see I am preparing a memorandum of this case which I hope to publish in time. My first contribution to the literature of crime. I thought if I could obtain such a startling piece of confirmation it would really make my name."

The old gentleman sighed.

"I'm very sorry," he said. "But I'm afraid I could not have my peaceful existence interrupted by a thing like that. I don't think we'll drag the pond," he added more firmly and for the first time Mr Stickles became uncomfortably aware that he was still holding the open razor. "And I don't think you'll complete your memorandum. You see, my mother was twenty-four years older than her youngest brother Brenner and was only twenty when I was born. I am the nephew."

→⇥⊩⊪← Murder in Reverse

The local doctor gave a certificate quite readily. So far as he was concerned, he said, there was nothing at all mysterious about the cause or circumstances of the man's death. Perhaps he should have been called in earlier, but even then it was not likely that he could have saved a life.

He had been summoned one evening by Mr. Whiston Grewer, who had recently come with his father, Hobart Grewer, to live at the Millhouse on the outskirts of the large village in which the doctor worked.

"It's old Wicks our manservant who is ill, doctor," said the voice on the telephone. "He has been suffering from anemia for some time but now he seems to be sinking."

When the doctor reached the Millhouse he was shown quickly to a little bedroom above the kitchen, reached by a separate staircase. Here he found a rather frail man in his sixties lying in bed.

He soon decided that Whiston Grewer was right. The patient was sinking fast.

"I know you'll do all you can for him," Whiston Grewer said. "He has been with us a long time and we're very fond of the old chap. My father gave him the chance of retiring two years ago and he refused because he wanted to go on looking after us."

Wicks died forty-eight hours later.

"Nothing odd about it," the doctor said to Detective-Sergeant Grebe, in answer to a query.

Yet Grebe remained obstinately dubious about the affair. The circumstances of life, if not of death, at the Millhouse were that the Grewers employed nobody in their household except Wicks, who had already been ailing when they arrived to take up residence ten days earlier. Whiston did the shopping and, apparently, most of the work of the house. Then had come the sudden worsening in the condition of Wicks, the summoning of the doctor and the seemingly natural death.

The body, Grebe learned, was to be cremated. The old man was a childless widower and had no living relative. There was a will leaving his savings, about £700, to the orphanage in which he had himself been brought up.

Within a week or two of the death of Wicks, a new staff appeared at the Millhouse. Whiston began to make friends in the district and entertained them rather lavishly. His father was rarely seen by the guests: he was reputed to be drinking too much.

About three years after the death of Wicks, the doctor was again called to the house, this time to attend Hobart Grewer, who was suffering from bronchitis.

"I've got to disappoint you again," he said to Grebe. "But once more this seems a perfectly ordinary illness."

"How is the son taking it?"

"Much as one would expect. He's anxious, but keeps pretty level-headed about it."

Grebe met the doctor one evening a fortnight later. "I've just arrested Whiston Grewer," he said.

"Then I think you've made a mistake. Which do you think he murdered, his father or Wicks?"

"Neither. I've arrested him for fraud."

"How's that?"

"It's the sort of crime that could belong only to our time," said Grebe, "when taxes and death duties and so on make people go to almost any length to avoid them. Hobart Grewer was a very rich man with liquid assets approaching six figures in value.

"Hoping to avoid paying death duties on this, Whiston persuaded his father to make over the bulk of it to him. But Hobart was an invalid and it soon began to seem unlikely that he would live the necessary five years which must elapse between a gift of this kind and the donor's death, if death duties are to be avoided.

"So Whiston took the precaution of moving his ailing father to a district in which neither he nor Wicks, the manservant, were known, and exchanging their identities.

"It was Hobart Grewer you attended during your first visits and Wicks who died the other day, quite naturally as Hobart had done. If his scheme had worked Whiston would have defrauded the country of a very large sum."

"But he wasn't a murderer?"

"No. A murderer in reverse. He kept his man alive. Fraudulently of course. He had no need to commit a murder. But I doubt whether I should have discovered the truth if I had not suspected him of one."

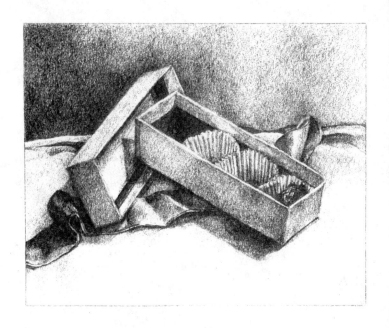

⇥║◄ Woman in the Taxi

"She's pale as a corpse," said the policeman, peering into the taxi.

"Well, that's not surprising," said the taxi driver, who had drawn up under the blue lamp of the police station. "She *is* a corpse. Why do you think I brought her here? If she was just sick I would have taken her to a hospital."

At the policeman's invitation, he went inside to make his statement. His name, it appeared, was Goddard Brown. He knew the woman who had been his fare, because she kept the fruit and flower shop opposite his usual stand and had more than once hired his cab to drive her home.

"She seemed a very nice person," he said. "Not over-generous with tips, but pleasant to speak to."

This evening she had left her shop with a man.

163

"What sort of a man? Oh, a big chap with a heavy moustache, dark hair, glasses, a black overcoat and a bowler hat."

The two had got in and Mrs Dolbick, the woman who was now dead, told Brown to drive to her home as usual. He started off, and as the glass between his seat and the cab interior was closed, he heard nothing of their conversation. He had noticed, however, as they had approached his cab, that the man was carrying a small packet.

After a while Brown was called on to stop. He did so, and the man alighted and, coming to the taximan's left side, gave him ten shillings and told him to take Mrs Dolbick home. It was not until he pulled up at her gate that Brown realised anything was wrong. As soon as he saw she was dead, huddled in her corner of the seat, he drove straight to the police station.

Detective-Sergeant Grebe, who was taking down these details, was handed a few papers and began to look through these while the taximan waited.

"I understand," he said at last, "that a small packet of chocolates has been found half empty beside the dead woman. Did you notice this?"

"Yes. When I discovered she was dead I saw it there. Thought I'd better leave it for you."

"Quite right. I needn't keep you now. We have your name and address. Thank you."

In the next few days the detective gathered some interesting information, but no clue as to the identity of the stranger described by the taxi-man. The chocolates, of a standard make, were examined and in each of the six that remained was found enough cyanide to kill a human being almost instantly, as it had certainly killed Mrs Dolbick.

Grebe then interviewed her husband, a small man, clean-shaven and fair, who wore light sporty clothes and a cloth cap and followed some mysterious calling connected with racing.

He seemed very upset by his loss, but admitted cheerfully, when asked by Grebe, that his wife's life was insured in his favour for £2000. The policy had been in force for a year. On the other hand, he said, her business and savings would go to her married daughter.

As for the stranger, he could suggest no one at all.

"My wife and I had our own lives, Inspector," he said candidly. "I didn't know all her friends nor she mine. I'm afraid I can't help you about this man. Some casual customer, perhaps, to whom she was giving a lift? Though he knew my wife well enough to be aware of one weakness of hers. Chocolates. She adored them."

Since Dolbick himself seemed to be the only man with any motive for the murder, Grebe checked on his movements at the time, but found, as he rather expected, that his alibi was cast-iron. He had been at Lingfield all day with a group of friends.

The inquest produced the expected verdict of willful murder by person or persons unknown, and for a time it looked as if the identity of Mrs Dolbick's poisoner would remain a mystery.

But Grebe, a patient man and a determined one, was waiting for a certain event. From the morning after the payment by the insurance company of the £2000 for which Mrs Dolbick's life was insured, her husband was followed by skilled and indefatigable shadows.

Their work did not last long. On the third day Grebe received the phone call he was expecting and drove down to Reading, from which town it had been made.

Grebe arrived in time to find Dolbick sitting comfortably in an armchair in one of the larger hotels. Beside him was the taxi-man. Within thirty hours they had been brought up before a magistrate on a joint charge.

"How did I know?" asked Grebe when a colleague pressed him. "I didn't, for certain. But I never quite believed in the stranger in the taxi. It struck me as odd when I met Dolbick that the stranger's description should have been precisely and in every respect the opposite to one of him, as though the man giving it wanted to make quite sure there was no confusion.

"Then those chocolates—one would have killed her, how could she have lived to eat half the box if the stranger had given it to her? Far more likely that a half-empty box had been put there deliberately as though the last fare had forgotten it. Mrs Dolbick's love for them would ensure the rest.

"It was a sordid little crime. The woman was murdered by these two acting in unison for a thousand pounds apiece. Neither would be suspected, they thought, for the husband had an alibi and the taxi-man no possible motive.

"An interesting thing and one which will get them convicted, I think, is their distrust of each other. How was Brown to be sure of collecting his half share? The answer is this piece of paper which was found on him when he went to meet Dolbick. *I promise to pay within three days of my receipt of £2000 from the Monumental Insurance Company £1000 of this in cash to Goddard Brown.*

"He must have hated writing that. But since Brown insisted on the security it gave him that he would not be bilked, what could Dolbick do?"

❧ The Nine-Fifty-Five

Frogmarsh kept perfectly cool. It was not the first time, he reminded himself, that a murderer had been alone in a house with the body of someone he had just killed. Others had lost their heads, tried to destroy the corpse by burning or even burying it. He had his plan worked out to the last detail.

He had waited a long time for tonight's combination of circumstances. It had to be a Tuesday, for it was on Tuesdays that old Mr Lloyd, his adopted father, took the evening train to pay his weekly visit to his office on the Wednesday. There had to be no one at home but the two of them. And—most important—it had to be a foggy night.

These three had come about this evening and one blow from a heavy club had ended Mr Lloyd's life so that Frogmarsh would come into possession of all that he coveted. There were no signs of a struggle, no evidence of his crime. Just the frail body of the old man neatly dressed in the suit he wore for his journey to London.

Frogmarsh finished his drink and cigarette and set to work. It was now just eleven o'clock and Mr Lloyd had been dead for nearly an hour.

First he went by the front door to where the car stood in the drive. He used no torch and did not switch on the light in the hall but proceeded by instinct and outstretched arm. He opened the rear door of the car and left it open while he went back to the house.

Then he put Mr Lloyd's heavy blue overcoat on the body, added the old man's bowler hat and brought his burden downstairs. Very gently and without haste he laid it in the back seat of the car.

He forgot nothing. Upstairs was the little attache case ready packed and he fetched it and put it beside the body. Mr Lloyd never carried an umbrella or Frogmarsh would have added that. Gloves were already attached to the dead hands.

Now, well wrapped up himself, he quietly

closed the front door and took the driving seat. The car started at a touch, and very slowly and cautiously, using only side-lights and trusting to his knowledge of every inch of the road, he drove off.

He passed nobody on his way to his destination. Not that it would have mattered. The fog was so thick that no car and certainly no driver would be recognisable.

When he stopped he took care that it was on the hard surface of the road so that no wheel-marks would be visible. He looked up to where the railway embankment looked over him, but the fog was too thick for its outline to be seen. This was the very spot, though, for he had carefully noted roadside objects to distinguish it.

There was not a sign or a sound of any living creature, and the nearest house was half a mile down the road. But now he faced his only risk, that of being seen while he actually carried the body to its resting-place. The risk was infinitesmal, but it had to be faced.

Quickly this time, he lifted the body, hurried to the foot of the slope and laid it sprawling head downwards on the ground. The hat he threw near it and the small bag he carried up the slope.

How could anyone, Frogmarsh asked himself, how could the cleverest detective in the world suspect that Mr Lloyd had not fallen or been pushed to his death from the 9:55 train that evening? The blow on the head might have been caused by his fall and Frogmarsh had seen to it that the body was bruised in places and the clothes disturbed and dirtied as they would have been in the fall.

Yes, he had thought of everything. Mr Lloyd had a season ticket, and the staff at Spincroft Junction could not possibly swear that he had not boarded his usual train. The carriage door could have swung itself shut if Mr Lloyd had fallen or jumped, or it could have been closed by his murderer if he had been pushed.

Frogmarsh himself had called on some friends at ten o'clock, having, he told them, just driven Mr Lloyd to the station as usual. Alibi, cause of death, disposal of body—all were perfectly accounted for.

He returned to his car. Still not a sight or sound. In a moment he was driving, always very cautiously, towards the house which would now be his. This time he put the car in the garage.

One last drink and Frogmarsh could forget his exertions in a peaceful night's sleep.

"A good job well done," he reflected as he looked out into the night before locking up. The fog showed signs of clearing. It might be days before the body was found.

He woke to find the weather only a little clearer. Downstairs he could hear the woman who came in every day to look after the two of them. He followed his usual routine till he was sitting by the fire with his coffee and newspaper.

He might, indeed have continued his day if it were not for a paragraph he found at the foot of a column. "Service Suspended. Owing to the dense fog the train service to London from Spincroft Junction was suspended after eight o'clock last night."

➤❚❮ Person or Persons

Mrs Tiggers was out of breath when she reached the police station. "Something's happened to Mr Holme," she said. "I've been knocking on his door for ten minutes and there's not a sound from inside."

"He may have gone away," the Station Sergeant pointed out.

"Well, he never has in all the years I've known him. And there was a light on in his cottage last night after eleven, because I saw it."

The Sergeant knew about Mr Holme. So did most people in the little town. An eccentric who lived alone and rarely spoke to anyone, he was reputed, like most lonely old men who live frugally, to be a miser and a misanthrope. The voluble Mrs Tiggers, who lived with her husband a few yards farther down the road, went in nearly every morning to "keep the place a bit decent," as she said.

"All right. I'll send someone round with you."

Accompanied by Constable Jevons, Mrs Tiggers returned to the little tumbledown house in which Mr Holme had lived alone for twenty years.

"Let's have a look round," Jevons said, when they had knocked more than once in vain.

It was a mock-Gothic cottage with pointed, diamond-paned windows, each protected by heavy bars. Jevons tried them all in turn, but could find no means of entry. The back door was firmly locked, and, from its tightness at top and bottom, seemed to be bolted as well. A very small bottle of milk was on the step.

"There was a man came to see him yesterday afternoon," remarked Mrs Tiggers. "Stranger to me. Stayed about half an hour and went off in a car."

"I shall have to break down this door," said Jevons.

Armed with a heavy log, he set about swinging it at the lock until, with a splintering sound, the door gave way.

They entered the small sitting-room on the

ground floor, which was dark and musty, and then looked in the kitchen. There was no sign of Mr Holme.

"Must be in his bedroom," said Mrs Tiggers. "This way."

The constable followed her up a steep little staircase and heard her screech as she opened a door at the top. Looking into the room over her shoulder he saw that the rafters were bare high above them and that hanging from a heavy beam which spanned the room was the little black-clad figure of Mr Holme. A chair was overturned at his feet.

Jevons said nothing, but quickly cut the rope and laid him on the bed.

"Been dead some time," he remarked to Mrs Tiggers.

"Whatever can have made him do it," she asked. "He didn't seem any different from any other time when I saw him yesterday. Poor old fellow."

Jevons looked carefully at the three windows on the upper floor and found them all tightly fastened from the inside.

"He did not mean to be disturbed," he remarked as they went downstairs.

Jevons got out his notebook and made a few inquiries of Mrs Tiggers, who had been joined by her husband, a man as quiet and stolid as she was excitable. She told Jevons what little she knew, but he explained that his questions were formal and that the matter would be more thoroughly dealt with later.

Back at the station he ran into Detective Sergeant Grebe and told him what he had found. He described the tightly closed cottage and the condition of the corpse, which was even now being examined by the doctor.

"Looks to me like quite an ordinary case of suicide," he said. "And from what I knew of the old chap he hadn't much to live for. Mrs Tiggers says he had a visitor yesterday afternoon, and that must be the first since he came here twenty years ago, according to all the reports. But there was one thing I noticed."

"Well?" asked Grebe.

"When I first broke in, there was a smell of tobacco smoke in the house. Old Holme was a heavy smoker, but he must have been dead for hours then."

Grebe looked up.

"We'll go and have a look round," he said.

They spent an hour in the cottage. Grebe examined very carefully the cubby-hole of a cloak-room where the dead man's one overcoat hung. He looked at the desk and found the papers in it arranged with a remarkable sense of order.

He went to the kitchen where the things on a tray showed that Holme's last meal had consisted of bread, margarine and fish paste while an uncut loaf argued a recent call from the baker. He examined the noose of the rope, the overturned chair, the dead man's pipe on the dressing-table.

"At what time does Mrs Tiggers say the stranger came yesterday?" he asked.

"Four o'clock. He stayed half an hour."

There was a long silence.

"I'll tell you what I think," said Grebe. "Holme was murdered. The motive was almost certainly the very simple and direct one of money he kept in the house. He was murdered last night by someone who remained here, probably concealed in the clothes cupboard by the front door, until you went upstairs — someone who could not resist smoking during the long time of waiting."

"Who?" asked Jevons inevitably.

"I've really told you. But here are some more facts about him. He knew where the money was hidden, since nothing in the whole place was disturbed by his search.

"He was probably known to the dead man since he was admitted last night without trouble. He knew he would be released from his vigil this morning and that you would be led upstairs when he got away.

"He was someone who could be seen round this house without causing comment. Someone, finally, who, rather than be seen leaving the cottage while you were upstairs, could be found by you arriving there when you came down."

"You mean Tiggers, of course."

"I mean Tiggers, but not alone. His wife's cooperation was essential, for it was she who knew where Holme's hoard was hidden, she who could raise the alarm in the morning and take the police upstairs while Tiggers left his hiding-place. She who could start a false scent or suggest some obscure reason for Holme's suicide by inventing a mysterious stranger, supposed to have called yesterday.

There's no proof yet, but we shall find that,
I'm pretty sure."

Grebe was right.

→❱❰← The Wrong Moment

Mr Minchin had good reason for wanting his wife out of the way. She was rich, fretful and selfish. She demanded endless attention and showed no gratitude for it. She was the most tactless creature in the world. Mr Minchin, himself a silky, diplomatic man, suffered endlessly from her habit of saying or doing the wrong thing at the wrong moment.

She lived an invalid's life, moving from English watering-place to Swiss mountain resort, and Mr Minchin had to accompany her. Wherever she went she could be relied on to choose someone's birthday party for a fit of depression, or to have a quarrel with her husband while they were dining with new friends, or to faint during church service.

She was also very sorry for herself, and frequently threatened to take her own life.

When they were first married and Albert

Minchin had heard her threatening—no, promising—to commit suicide, it had raised his hopes. He knew to a penny the sum he would receive on Gracie Minchin's death.

He sighed. "Independent," he thought. No more coddling this crotchety and self-pitying woman. No more of her fortune spent on specialists and nursing homes. He would be a free and prosperous man.

He started encouraging her. He would leave her alone in her hotel bedroom with a supply of sleeping tablets. He took her for a holiday to Beachy Head and let her go for walks alone along the cliffs. He arranged for them to spend some weeks together on a cruise and talked kindly and convincingly of the beautiful peace that was to be found in death by drowning.

All in vain. Gracie went on saying that she did not wish to live, that she would be better out of the way, that she longed to be dead. But she made no effort to achieve it.

"I shall do it one of these days," she said. "What have I got to live for? You only married me for my money."

"You musn't say that."

"Well, it's true."

It was, of course.

He had always been very careful. When he had given Gracie those little opportunities he had made sure that he was well out of the way at the time when she might be taking advantage of them. He had every motive for murdering her, as anyone could see. It must be a plain open-and-shut case of suicide or nothing at all.

Now they were renting a furnished flat, over-looking a seaside town. It was winter. One evening she was more than usually exasperating. She had been querulous all day and now objected to his going out for a walk alone.

"You leave me alone here for hours on end. You have no consideration for me at all."

"Nonsense. I've been running about for you all day."

He was standing in front of her, trying to keep his temper.

"There's no need to shout."

"I'm not shouting."

"I know you. You only married me for my money."

Suddenly Albert could control himself no longer. He raised his arm and struck his wife in the face. Horrified he watched her sink into a chair.

When he found that she had really fainted, he went for water and brought her round. Her face was growing scarlet and puffy where his blow had landed.

"You brute," she whined. "You cowardly brute! You'll be sorry for this. I'm going to bed. You can go out—I hope you do. I don't want you near me after that. Yes, go out and stay out!"

Albert did. But first he went into her bedroom and pocketed the sleeping tablets. Never do for her to take too many now and be found with the mark of his blow on her face. Then he watched while she entered the bedroom and, satisfied that she was going to bed, he marched off slamming the front door behind him.

He realised that he would have to wait now before even giving her another opportunity of doing what she threatened, and this time he would have to think of some way to make her take that opportunity. He began to consider this as he walked along the windswept empty sea front.

It was three hours before he returned to the flat and as he entered it he could immediately smell gas. He opened the landing window before he cautiously entered Gracie's room. She was dead.

They took him in for questioning next day.

"Of course she did it herself," he pleaded. "She was always threatening to commit suicide."

"People who threaten very rarely carry it out," said the detective.

"Well, she did. I tell you I went for a walk and when I came back I found her there."

"What about that bruise on her face?"

"I did that. I admit it. I lost my temper. It had nothing to do with the other thing."

"No? The doctor thinks it was done a few minutes before your wife lost consciousness.

"We think your wife was murdered, Mr Minchin. Struck senseless, then placed in the bedroom with the gas turned on to look like suicide. All the evidence points to that. Now can you account for your movements at the time?"

"I went for a walk."

"At what time?"

"About nine."

"And returned at midnight? You were walking about for three hours?"

"I was thinking. I'm afraid appearances are against me."

"They are, Mr Minchin."

"But why, why should she have chosen tonight of all nights, the only time I ever struck her, to do what she was always threatening to do?"

The detective, a cold and skeptical man, did not seem interested.

So Albert Minchin was tried, condemned and hanged. And all—as he protested to the end— because his wife had characteristically chosen the wrong moment.

➤✦◄ A Box of Capsules

It was the old doctor's warning which had first given Miss Hipton the idea.

"Take care of these capsules," he said. "Never more than one at a time. Too many could be fatal."

She nodded and looked serious, but secretly she was irritated. Why should the doctor, of all people, be so vague about quantity? "Too many" would be fatal. But how many? She did not even know what poison the capsules contained. When the time came she would just have to guess what made an overdose.

"I hope Mrs Lane will soon feel relief," said the doctor.

"She will," said Miss Hipton.

That was two years ago. The old doctor had died soon after his last visit and the capsules had diminished one by one in the prescribed doses, but still Miss Hipton had waited her time. There would be no point in taking the opportunity provided until the last will and testament of Mrs Lane had been signed. For the last five of the twelve years during which she had been the old lady's companion, that had been promised to her.

She looked back over those twelve years of ministering to a rich, bad-tempered old woman, twelve years of forced smiles and thoughtful gestures on a pittance, twelve years of humil-iation.

But they were ended now. Only last week she had seen the document for which she waited. It was signed and witnessed now. "The residue to my faithful friend and companion, Eleanor Hipton, if still in my service."

And then . . . Miss Hipton stared out of the window as if she could see as far as the holiday resort at which she had met Alban Baintree. She would join him at Eastmouth and they could spend the rest of their lives indulging in the hobby which had brought them together.

Photography had been her passion since child-hood. When she had met Alban Baintree, she had found in him an enthusiast as devoted as she was. The letters they exchanged were not frequent, but there was an excellent under-standing between them. They would wait till Mrs Lane had "passed on" (as Miss Hipton put it) and then marry and start a business together.

Miss Hipton reflected that she owed Alban a letter now. She would not, of course, speak of her immediate plan, or give the least hint that the event they awaited was about to take place, sooner than was natural. She wrote of everyday things, of her longing to see Alban, and then as usual of their hobby. She told him that she had been able to obtain the stuff needed for inten-sifying certain negatives and that he could ex-pect results from it soon. She signed herself, "Your devoted Eleanora."

Then she went up to the bedroom in which Mrs Lane was lying. "In pain again, dear?" she said. "I'm so sorry. I've got some new cap-sules the doctor sent."

"Capsules," moaned Mrs Lane. "I'm sick of their capsules. They don't seem to help at all."

"These will, I'm sure," said Miss Hipton. "I'll leave them beside you tonight. You can take as many as you wish."

Miss Hipton went cheerfully to bed. Tomor-row, with any luck, she would be free.

In the morning Mrs Lane was dead with the empty capsule box beside her. Soon Miss Hipton was explaining everything to the young doctor who had taken Dr Morlock's practice.

"I've always been afraid of something like this," said Miss Hipton. "The pain must have been just too much for her and she decided to bear it no longer. She has swallowed all the capsules in the box."

"What capsules?" said the doctor.

"Oh, those Dr Morlock gave her two years ago. She knew perfectly well that more than one at a time was dangerous."

Miss Hipton was not worried when she heard there was to be a post-mortem. They would find the poison but there could be no suggestion that it was anything but self-administered.

It was not until after her arrest that she realised what had happened. As she heard in the police court the evidence collected against her, it dawned on her that the drug used in Dr Morlock's capsules and the chemical she had bought for intensifying her photographs were the same—potassium bichromate. An old-fashioned way of treating a gastric ulcer, it seemed, which few modern doctors recommended. But no one believed at all in the existence of the capsules when Miss Hipton's last letter to Alban Baintree was read out— that carefully innocent letter which she had written discreetly on the eve of Mrs Lane's death.

"I've got the stuff," she wrote. "I did not even have to sign the poison book. It's called potassium bichromate, it seems, and can't fail in its purpose. You may therefore expect some startling developments soon. Oh, my dear, I am looking forward so much to the time when we shall be together for good."

⇥❈❈⇤ Blind Witness

It looked a particularly brutal murder. Adam Mufflin, an elderly widower, was found dead at the foot of the cliffs near the fishing village of Alderstone. Apparently he had been struck on the head while taking his brother Abel, a blind cripple, for his usual afternoon outing in a wheelchair on the footpath along the cliffs. After the attack the body had been pushed over the edge.

The two old brothers were well-known local characters who lived together in the village. Adam was believed to be well-off. Abel had lost his sight when he was seventeen and had become a cripple more recently. For all his disabilities he was a cheerful, talkative man who liked to have people around him.

The two brothers were devoted to each other. They kept a car, specially constructed so that

Abel's wheel-chair could be carried in it, and they had a chauffeur named Blickton who had been with them for years. Adam insisted that he himself should wheel his brother every day. He had done this for three years, ever since the sudden paralysis which had robbed Abel of all power of movement in his legs.

On the afternoon of the murder they had left the house as usual, having arranged that Blickton should meet them with the car at a point two miles along the cliff. They had seemed very cheerful as they set off.

It was Adam's son, Cyril, who had later found the cripple alone in his wheel-chair at a point where a slight dip in the cliffs rendered the edge invisible from a distance. The old man was in a terrible state of baffled incoherence.

He described how his brother had left him for a moment to dig up a few cowslip roots with a trowel he carried. "I heard him go some paces away and heard the sound of his trowel," said Abel. "Then there was a thud."

Abel's hearing was acute but the soft grass muffled the sound of most movements. He thought he heard dragging footsteps in the direction of the cliff's edge. He shouted his brother's name again and again but received no answer.

The blind man had heard nothing which might give a clue to the assailant's identity.

The police looked first for a possible motive. They found that Abel was the main beneficiary under Adam's will since Adam had made over a large sum of money to his son six years ago to avoid death duties. Cyril, however, was named in the will. Two thousand pounds went to Blickton and there were smaller bequests.

Cyril and Blickton were both questioned. Cyril lived in London and had been summoned by telegram to come and see his father that day. He had wired in reply that he would arrive on the 2:17, and had done so, reaching the house just after the two brothers had set out.

"I knew their usual route," he said, "and followed them. I must have arrived too late, for I never saw my father alive again."

Blickton said: "I drove the car to the point where the cliff footpath joins the road and waited there. I smoked two cigarettes. I heard and saw nothing till Mr Cyril brought Mr Abel along in his wheelchair."

Sergeant Grebe of the local CID made a careful examination of the place where Adam was attacked. He found the weapon—a poker which lay near by—and there were no finger-prints on it. The poker came from the house. He also found that the grass had been flat-tened—not for the width of a foot or so, as it would have been if Adam's unconscious body had been dragged to the cliff edge, but for about five feet, as though the unconscious man had been rolled there. He also found some blood-stains which showed him that a blow had indeed been struck as Abel said, before Adam, already dead or unconscious, had been pushed from the edge.

Finally Grebe examined the wheelchair and discovered bloodstains on this, too.

"Interesting," said Grebe to one of his col-leagues before making the arrest. "You will notice that neither of the two suspects had a satisfactory alibi and neither of them seems to have bothered about one. If there is an alibi here it was prepared three years before the murder."

"Three years?" said the colleague.

"Yes. At the time when Abel Mufflin became paralysed. That gave him a perfect alibi. Oh yes, he was blind all right. Nothing faked about that. But he had only been blind since the later years of a boyhood spent in this district. He knew every inch of the cliff footpath.

"A patient man, he let his rich, devoted brother wheel him about for three years until his inability even to stand up was an established fact. Then he phoned a wire to Cyril to bring him in-to the district at the right time that afternoon and arranged that Blickton, too, would be a suspect.

"We shall never know, of course, how he got his brother in range of the poker he had concealed under his rug. Perhaps he asked to stop at that point and knew just where Adam's head would be while he was putting a wedge under the wheel of the chair. But if his account were true and Adam was hit while a few paces away, why were there bloodstains on the wheelchair? And why was the body rolled to the cliff edge, unless it was by a blind man, feeling his way?

"Motive? Adam gave him everything he wanted. There are people who would rather commit a murder than live on charity."

→╫← Deceased Wife's Sister

"Don't look at me like that, Gilbert," said Mrs Runshore. "Anybody would think you were going to kill me!"

"I am," replied her husband and proceeded to do so, quietly and efficiently, leaving no trace of bloodshed in the tiled bathroom.

Then he put the rest of his plan into operation.

"Method," he had often said to his untidy wife. "Method in all things."

In murder, too, he reflected now, method and a cool head were the two essentials. For instance there was her bag to pack. If she had indeed left him suddenly to join that farmer they had met on holiday last year, as Gilbert Runshore would certainly maintain she had done, there would be a number of things she would not have left behind.

It was his business to know every one of them

and put them in her suitcase so that the most inquisitive examiner could search the house without finding evidence that Mrs Runshore herself had not packed.

He consulted the list he had prepared. Clothes, jewellery, mother's photograph, compact, new shoes—he forgot nothing. She would only have taken what she could carry herself, so he was spared the puzzle of selecting many clothes. Books? She scarcely ever read. Perfume? She did not like it. He was soon able to fasten the catch of her bag.

Now came the exertion of carrying the body to the garage and concealing it under rugs in the back of the car. His wife had never been heavy and the burden was soon carried. The suitcase followed. Now Gilbert Runshore started his long night's drive.

That old mine-shaft was an inspiration. He could drive up to it unobserved, drop the body and suitcase at a certain point he had noticed and be sure that they would fall into the black depths to lie undiscovered for years.

"Or even centuries," he chuckled, imagining some prospector or archaeologist coming on a crumbling skeleton long after he himself would be no more than dust.

The mineshaft had another advantage. It was over a hundred miles from his home and only three from the house in which the farmer—that friend of his wife's—lived alone.

If by some freak of chance the body was discovered earlier than he supposed, who could say that Effie Runshore had not gone to the farmer and been murdered by him?

When he had driven some twelve miles through the darkness, he pulled into a lonely by-road and removed the number-plates of his car, replacing them with the old set he had kept ready. This little feat he had rehearsed several times and could achieve in less than ten minutes. The chances were ten to one against his number-plates being observed in the region of the mineshaft, but ten to one was not good enough for him. He wanted a thousand to one against discovery.

All went according to schedule: the corpse was dropped and so was the suitcase; the return journey was made without incident; the original number-plates were replaced and the false ones thrown in a wayside pond. Not a detail was forgotten.

Even when, the next afternoon, he looked out of the window and saw his sister-in-law, Beryl Forkley, marching up to the front door, he was not unduly alarmed. Beryl was a downright observant woman, but everything was ready for her most searching questions or discoveries. Gilbert Runshore guessed that Effie must have asked her to come and decided that this could well be turned to confirmation of the story he had prepared.

"She cannot have been quite as heartless as I supposed," he said after explaining that his wife had left him. "At least she thought of me alone in the house and incapable of management. She sent you to look after me."

"She said nothing about it," said Beryl sharply. "She just asked me to stay for a few days. I expected to find her here."

"I wish you could," sighed Gilbert Runshore. "I can still scarcely believe she had left me to go to that farmer we met last year."

All that afternoon and evening Beryl continued to ask questions, which, however, her brother-in-law was able to answer quite readily. Why had Effie not taken her green dress? How did Gilbert know where she had gone? What train did she take?

But when Beryl came down next morning there were no more questions, or, in fact, much conversation between them at all. Beryl looked grim and watched Gilbert suspiciously as he tried to behave with calm and detachment.

After breakfast she hurried out, and in half an hour was sitting in front of a detective-inspector in the local police station.

"I can't, of course, be sure of where you'll find the body, but I think it may be at the bottom of an old mineshaft at a place called Bidleigh," she finished, after giving details about her suspicions.

"And what first made you think your sister had been murdered?" asked the detective-inspector.

"At first I merely thought it odd that she should have gone away without telling me. Not that she should have left Gilbert—nothing odd about that: she ought to have done it years ago. But she would have told me what she was doing.

"It was when I slept in her room that I became certain. You see, there was something about Effie that her husband did not know. She was an inveterate, a wildy enthusiastic diarist. She had kept her journal for years."

"You mean you had read what she had written lately and found that her husband had made previous attempts?"

"Not at all. It was nothing that I read which made me suspect. The diary gave me the idea of the mineshaft because Effie described their finding it and mentioned Gilbert's remark that it would be a good place to conceal a body. But you don't know much about women, Inspector, if you don't see why that diary made me suspicious."

"Well?"

"The fact that apparently she had left it behind, of course, hidden in its usual place behind the books on the shelf. Would any woman leaving her husband forget to pack that, do you think? As soon as I saw it I knew that Gilbert had put the things in her bags, not Effie, and that he knew nothing of the diary.

"And you don't know much about diarists either if you think one of them would go away and leave a half-written diary. I didn't need to read it. The fact that it was there started me thinking and will eventually hang Gilbert, I believe."

➤➤❤❤ Riverside Night

"There's a dead man in the kitchen!" cried Mrs Watworth, bursting into the sitting-room of her riverside cottage.

"Please don't come in without knocking," replied her lodger severely. "There is nothing whatever to be excited about. The cadaver will be removed as soon as it is dark this evening."

"You mean. . . ." Mrs Watworth was aghast.

"I mean that I have unfortunately been forced to eliminate this man. He was attempting to blackmail me."

"He was a bus-conductor, wasn't he?" asked Mrs Watworth, trying to recover herself. The first thing she had noticed that evening was the round disc of his white cap-cover where the peaked cap hung on a hook by the dresser.

"That happened to be his occupation," said Mr Sitchwell dryly. "He was also an unpleasant and dangerous man. I am sorry that his corpse should be infesting your kitchen, but in a couple of hours I shall row it out to midstream and dispose of it. There will be nothing whatever to connect his disappearance with me or you or this house."

"But . . . but Mr Sitchwell, it's murder!"

"Technically it might be called that. I prefer to think of it as mercy killing."

"I ought to go to the police."

"If I thought you were serious, Mrs Watworth, I should feel bound to dispose of two corpses this evening. Fortunately I know you to be a sensible woman. You may go now. Perhaps it would be as well if you remained upstairs until your kitchen has been cleared of refuse."

Mrs Watworth did as suggested, retiring to her bedroom and locking the door. She had always thought her lodger was odd in his behaviour, but now she believed him to be stark mad. She quickly decided what she must do. She dare not move while Mr Sitchwell was in the house but as soon as he had taken that horrible corpse to the boat-house and rowed away, she would telephone for the police.

Presently she heard her lodger calling her.

"I'm going now," he said. "I shan't be very long. In case you should be tempted to tell anyone what you believe you have seen, let me warn you that I have already reported that you suffer from delusions. No one will believe that a dead bus-conductor was lying on your kitchen floor, and long before the man is missed or his body recovered I shall have disappeared as inconspicuously as I came. So just have your supper quietly and go to bed. You won't regret it."

Mrs Watworth stood silent and horror-struck while Mr Sitchwell picked up the dead man and went out by the back door. It was very dark and she could not see him clearly as he made for the boat-house, but listening she heard the door squeak and then the sound of the boat being taken out. Finally she could hear the splash of oars.

She rushed to the telephone and was soon gasping frenzied words into the instrument.

"Murder, I tell you. He's taking him out now in a boat to get rid of him. He's mad, I think. Yes, I saw the dead man on my kitchen floor!"

It seemed to her that the police promised

almost reluctantly to come round. She had the feeling that she was not believed. But she sat down to wait for the sound of the police car in the road outside.

Half an hour passed, then Mrs Watworth heard the boat returning before the car. Mr Sitchwell walked in smiling.

"There!" he said. "Soon done, wasn't it? Since you haven't gone to bed, what about a nice cup of tea?"

He seemed perfectly good-humored even when, ten minutes later, the car at last drew up and a sergeant and constable were admitted.

Mrs Watworth almost fell on them.

"He's a murderer!" she screamed. "He has killed a man who was blackmailing him and dropped his body in the river. I saw it lying in the kitchen."

"Now, now. . ." said the sergeant soothingly and turned to Mr Sitchwell. "What does she mean?" he asked.

Mr Sitchwell appeared unruffled.

"Poor lady. She has been having these little attacks lately. I'm afraid she needs a doctor more than the police. I don't know a live bus-conductor, let alone a dead one."

The sergeant remained cool.

"You are quite sure of what you say?" he asked Mrs Watworth.

She tried to answer calmly, but she was half in tears and growing hysterical.

"Of course I am. It was lying on the floor. He told me he'd killed him. You'll find the corpse in the river. You're not to leave me alone with him. I tell you he's a murderer!"

Mr Sitchwell sighed.

"No need to worry about leaving her alone with me," he said in a man-to-man way to the police. "I can go round to the hotel for the night. But I think this lady needs care."

Mrs Watworth thought she was going to faint. Then drifting through her misty mind came a white disc, like the moon among clouds. A white disc—a white cap cover.

"Look!" she cried, pointing wildly to it, where it still hung on the hook by the dresser.

Then she must have fainted.

She recovered, however, long before the trial; and she gave evidence for the successful prosecution.

Rufus— and the Murderer

"That's our mascot," said Detective-Sergeant Brent. "We call him Rufus. He helped us to convict a murderer once. We're very fond of him." He pointed to a life-sized dummy hanging on a peg in a corner of his office. His visitor saw a white blank where the face should have been, a battered hat, an old blue suit, all apparently filled with stuffed sacking. There was something grotesque about this. It had the horror of a realistic scarecrow seen by a child.

"How did that happen?" the visitor asked, not very willingly.

Detective-Sergeant Brent told the story.

About two years ago (he said) we had a man living here called Basil Ragley. He was a rich man whose wife had left him and he was drinking too much. His brother was a local farmer who was jealous because Basil had inherited and improved their father's business, while he, Cyril, had nothing but a none-too-prosperous farm.

Basil had bought a big house called Miller's End, which stands at the foot of the gorge. In this hilly country, houses seem to have been built too high or too low on the mountainside. Miller's End is low and approached by a road which winds steeply downwards from the outskirts of this town.

Every night Basil drove home in his big Daimler and everyone warned him that he would kill himself. He did not get drunk, but he drank too much, if you understand me. He was lit, he was oiled, but he was never intoxicated. He swung his great car round the bends of that road with a 200-foot drop beside him. It frightened people.

It did not frighten the brother, though. Cyril Ragley heard about these drives home with pleasurable anticipation. One night, he hoped, the predicted accident would happen and he would wake up to find himself a rich man.

But years began to pass and Basil grew less nervy and depressed and even started to cut down his drinking. This alarmed Cyril, whose prospect of premature inheritance was fading.

He decided to assist what he felt was the course of nature. He made up his mind to wait for an accident no longer.

It had to be carefully done, for if there was anything to show it was murder he would be the only suspect. No one else had a motive for killing Basil.

On the other hand, he thought, with that big car going down a most dangerous slope every night it ought not to be too difficult to avoid all suspicion of what the newspapers called "foul play."

His difficulty was to stop the Daimler on its way home at night, somewhere high on the hill where the decline was steep. It was for this purpose that he thought of Rufus. A man lying in the middle of the road—Basil was sure to stop. For one thing the road was so narrow that he could not avoid it. For another, he was the sort of man who would stop for anyone in trouble.

It would all be simple, Cyril thought. A dummy in the road, a squeak of brakes, Basil leaning over the dummy in the headlights of his car, a crack from behind with a padded knob-kerrie, Basil's body, unconscious or dead, put back in the driving seat of the car, and the handbrake released.

Cyril would be able to stand there and listen to the delightful sound of the Daimler crashing down the first little slope, then bouncing its way with loud reverberations to the foot of the gorge.

Who could suggest foul play then? It would be an accident, pure and simple.

He meanwhile would take Rufus and make his way quietly home across the fields. They might suspect that the fall had not been entirely accidental. They might even think he had something to do with it. They could never prove anything. A tragic accident, no more.

It all worked out admirably. He hid behind some trees while his dummy was stretched across the road. His brother's car came veering down and stopped, its headlights on the dummy. He smashed his life-preserver down as Basil bent over the dummy, then bundled his brother into his driving seat. He watched the car slide forward, gather speed and eventually leap into space, as it seemed, when it left the road.

Then the crashes, one after another as the car

seemed to bounce. These, he thought, were disappointingly remote, almost muffled. There was no explosion. But never mind—his object was achieved. Basil was dead and in a few moments cremated as the car burst into flames at the foot of the gorge.

As he turned back to pick up his dummy and make his secret way home he saw the lights of another car descending the hill. It had not occurred to him that Basil might have asked some casually met acquaintances to follow him home.

Cyril had followed the Daimler for a few paces and now had no time to pick up his dummy without being seen. He had to leave it there as he dived into the hedge.

The second car stopped as Basil's had. Two men alighted to examine the dummy. They chuckled when they saw what it was, and, calling back to another member of the party who had remained in the car that it was some gag of Basil's, they picked the thing up.

It was only as they drove away with it that Cyril realised that his number was up.

"You mean you got a conviction?" said Brent's visitor.

"Rufus got it, I think," replied Detective-Sergeant Brent. "Cyril was tough at first and if he had refused to admit anything we might never have been able to charge him. But we found that we only had to have Rufus in the room to get a statement. The sight of Rufus nodding down to him from that peg set Cyril confessing almost too eagerly. It was rather gruesome, really."

"But how did you know it was his in the first place?"

"Oh, that. It was too simple. An insult to a good detective. He never supposed that anyone would see Rufus except himself and Basil. He dressed him in his own old suit."

⇢⊪⊫⊰ The Marsh Light. . .

It was for help, not to give information, that Mr Boyd Lucaster went to the police station. But something he said to the desk sergeant caused him to be referred to the CID. He was sitting now with Detective-Sergeant Grebe, who was in charge here.

Mr Boyd Lucaster was naturally a chatty man.

"We climbed Winlock Fell today," he said proudly. "My nephew Simon and I. Not bad going because I shall be sixty-five next month."

"Very good," said Grebe.

"We started out at six o'clock this morning but even so it had grown dusk before we came down the east side of the mountain. It was quite dark when we came to the marshy land at the foot."

"Marshy land! There's about four square miles

of bog there. Dangerous country."

"So my nephew said. He knows the district well, you see. Stays here every year. He told me today that there had been more lives lost through that bog than through all the climbing in the whole area."

"He's probably right."

"However, he knew the way across it perfectly. It was made more complicated by the fact that, as you know, many tracks and paths that are used for years suddenly sink or become lost. You may be following one that looks safe and firm to you, and suddenly find yourself swallowed up."

"I know," said Grebe. "It happens every year."

"We must have come about a mile, and now it was quite dark. We were walking in single file because my nephew said that was safest. There was a little moonlight now and again, but not enough to depend on. We had just passed the little copse—"

"Which little copse?"

"I only saw one. Bligh's Copse, my nephew called it."

"I know."

"Suddenly my nephew gave a cry and fell. His foot had been caught by a root or something, and his momentum was sufficient for him to be thrown to the ground."

"Bad luck, that," said Grebe.

"I helped him to his feet, but he had given his ankle a terrible sprain. He tried to hobble on it but could not. We were in a very difficult position. He could not move his foot at all after a few moments. What was I to do?"

"Just what you did, of course. Leave him there and look for help."

"Help? But it was almost certain that I could find no one this side of the village of Bligh Abbott and that was two miles away. And I privately doubted whether I should ever reach it.

"My nephew gave me the most careful instructions. Continue on that track for five hundred yards, he said. There would probably be a light visible on the right which I was to ignore. But at a fork there I was to take the left track and walk for another mile, which would bring me in sight of the village.

"I set out as he told me, actually counting my paces to know when I had gone five hundred yards. And there, sure enough, was the light. It was much nearer than I supposed and to the right of the track.

"Just then the moon came out and I was almost certain that where the light was shining I recognised the shape of a building, while from the point at which I was standing a cart-track was visible, leading towards it. I had heard of marsh lights and illusions in country like this but I felt sure this was not one of them.

"But I remembered my nephew's instructions. Ignore the light, he had said, and take the left fork when you come to it. How could I do otherwise than obey that? Just then, however, the moon came out again and I strained my eyes towards the light. Now I was sure. There was the distinct shape of a cottage and the clear parallel lines of a cart-track going towards it. I resolved to follow them.

"The track was perfectly good. I soon found myself at the door of the cottage, and knocked.

"I found an excellent chap called Rivers, who at once volunteered to see me safely to Bligh Abbott. We reached it half an hour later, and Rivers arranged for some men to go out and bring my nephew in. When my nephew arrived we came in to this town by taxi. We're staying at the Bligh Arms."

"What brought you to the police station, Mr Lucaster?"

"Oh, that. Yes." He was pulling out pen and cheque book. "I had no money on me. I am leaving tomorrow. I wanted you to arrange for a little award to those who helped us."

Grebe was thoughtful.

"Tell me," he said at last. "When Rivers was leading you to the village did he take the way your nephew had given you?"

"No. I noticed that. When we came to the fork he took the path to the right."

"I see. How has your nephew behaved today? Anything odd in his manner?"

"There was one small thing. He had a little fall as we were on our way home. The merest little slide down a slope. But after that he became very reserved. And whereas he had been leading all day, he now insisted on walking behind."

"Did he give any explanation of that?"

"None."

"Did you pass anyone?"

"Yes. A farmer called Tom Harris. My

nephew knew him."

"What doctor has attended your nephew this evening?"

"He did not want to see one, but I insisted. I telephoned to a Dr Bridges and left him with him."

Grebe dialed a number. Perplexed but interested, Mr Lucaster heard him ask for Dr Bridges, then put some questions about Simon Lucaster's sprained ankle. Mr Lucaster could not hear the reply but, watching Grebe's face, thought he saw its expression change to one of surprise.

There was silence for a moment. Then Grebe picked up the receiver and dialed again. This time he enquired from the landlord of the King's Arms if Tom Harris was in the bar. Apparently he was, for soon Grebe was asking him if he remembered seeing two men on Winlock Fell. Again the reply was inaudible to Mr Lucaster but it seemed to interest Grebe.

Finally Grebe turned again to Mr Lucaster.

"I must ask you, I'm afraid, whether your nephew has any interest in your estate. Would your death benefit him?"

"Oh yes. He is, in fact, my sole heir."

Grebe nodded.

"This evening," he said seriously, "I believe he tried to murder you."

"Really! But—"

"I am speaking quite unofficially, of course. I doubt if there will be any evidence for a prosecution. But I don't think you should go climbing with your nephew again. If you had followed the instructions he gave you tonight you would have gone straight to your death. He knew that perfectly well."

"Are you sure?"

"I'm afraid so. The piece of bogland reached by the left fork is the most dangerous in the district. Your nephew was in a search party last year when a man lost his life there. He was deliberately sending you into it."

Mr Lucaster blinked.

"You mean his sprained ankle was a fake?"

"I admit I thought that at first. If it had been, we should have been able to obtain a conviction for attempted murder. But I was mistaking effect for cause. His sprain was perfectly genuine. Quite a bad one, in fact."

"But surely that exonerates him?"

"No," said Grebe.

"What did you mean when you said that you were mistaking effect for cause?"

"Just this. It was when he sprained his ankle that he saw his opportunity. It gave him his idea. The sprain wasn't part of the plot; the plot was a result of the sprain. He did not sprain it down in the bog but up on the mountain. You noticed his silence after that little fall. He was in pain. He was also thinking out his plan."

"But how do you know this?" asked Mr Lucaster.

"He asked you to go in front, didn't he? Single file? Why do you think that was? I heard from Tom Harris just now.

"When he saw you both this afternoon your nephew was walking behind. He was limping."

→❱❚❬← A Stiff Drink

"Drink up," said Mr Birdlock, "it'll do you good." His cheerful prediction was scarcely justified because a moment later his companion swallowed some of his whisky and soda and fell dead on the floor of the saloon bar.

In the scene which followed Mr Birdlock appeared more bewildered than frightened.

"Can't make it out," he kept repeating. "Poor old Ruffins. Seemed quite cheerful when we came in. I haven't known him long. Seemed a good chap. Can't make it out."

The police, however, were less at a loss. In the small quantity of whisky-and-soda remaining in the broken glass from which Ruffins had drunk, they found cyanide of potassium. There seemed on the face of it, to be two possibilites—that the man had committed suicide or that Birdlock was a murderer.

The bottle from which Miss Ames the glittering barmaid had poured the whisky and the siphon from which it had been diluted were examined and contained nothing noxious.

"Yet," said Detective-Sergeant Grebe, "I should not have thought he was a man to commit suicide and I can't see Birdlock as a murderer."

So he began his usual patient investigation.

He discovered that the dead man was one of three brothers and that the two who survived him were both local tradesmen, Alfred Ruffins a chemist, and Duggan Ruffins a printer. He discovered moreover that the dead man Horace Ruffins had two characteristics well known to his associates, characteristics which are rarely found in the same person: he was a heavy drinker and he was mean to the point of miserliness.

Of Mr Birdlock who had accompanied him that evening to the pub, Grebe discovered very little. He had not lived long in the town and put up at the same boarding-house as Horace Ruffins. He had no visible occupation but paid his lodgings regularly and seemed a respectable person.

Grebe questioned Birdlock closely about the

few minutes just before Ruffins fell dead.

"I met him in the street," he said. "I think it was he who suggested that we should go and have one. He seemed very pleased with himself. Chuckling and grinning as we went into the bar. But he didn't say very much. When I said I could only stop for one he laughed and said: I only need one. Just like that. 'I only need one.' Funny thing to say because he showed no signs of having had a drink and it was only just after opening time. He seemed delighted about it though. That's all I remember."

"Who bought the drinks?"

"I did. But it was usually the other way. He knew I drink light ale and he whisky so he would make a little investment to bring him interest when I bought the second round. He didn't offer me a drink when we came in. And there wasn't a second round," ended Mr Birdlock rather solemnly.

"You did not tamper with his drink?"

"Certainly not."

"And you did not see him put anything into it?"

"No. But I left him for a moment to speak to a man I know."

Detective-Sergeant Grebe liked his two alternatives less and less. What motive could there be in either case? Ruffins was a glutton for life, the last man who would want to quit it. Birdlock could gain nothing by his death.

"Yet someone put cyanide in his whisky," Grebe reflected. "And the only people who had access to it were Ruffins, Birdlock and Miss Ames. Birdlock says he watched the barmaid as she poured. He even saw her give the glasses a last polish before using them.

He decided to investigate the two brothers of the dead man. They after all were the only people he knew of who might have a motive since Horace Ruffins left a nice round sum of money and had no other relatives. But he drew a blank here.

The chemist had not been on speaking terms with his brother Horace for some time, had not supplied him with anything for more than a year and called his assistant to witness these facts. Moreover he had never been known to enter the pub in which the death had occurred.

The printer had seen the late Horace for a moment in the street that afternoon, but had been up in London at the relevant time.

Then Grebe went to the boarding-house in which the late Horace Ruffins and Mr Birdlock both lived and interviewed the proprietress. It appeared that he was not the first to be interested in the dead man's belongings.

"His brother has been here this morning," said the proprietress. "Mr Duggan Ruffins, I mean. He's an executor and he was looking for a certain paper, he said. Something to do with the will."

"Did he find it?"

"No, but you should see the mess he's left things in. Drawers turned inside out and papers all over the place."

Detective-Sergeant Grebe, however, had more practice in searching and after about thirty minutes opened a novel from the library and whistled as he removed a small piece of paper which had been put in as a bookmark. Then he went back to the station to apply for a warrant.

"Well," said the superintendent. "Which was it, Birdlock or suicide?"

"Neither."

"It was murder?"

"Yes."

"The chemist brother?"

"No. The printer. I worked it out this way. If the barmaid and Birdlock were innocent Ruffins must have poisoned his own whisky. If he was not a suicide he did not know what he was putting in. But he must have had some reason for putting it in. What reason could he have had? The answer was in his last words—I only need one. That sentence gave me my clue. Ruffins must have meant something by that. The only interpretation I could make linked it up nicely with the poison—he believed that what he put in his drink would make any more expense on alcohol unnecessary that evening. A strengthener of some sort."

The Superintendent smiled grimly.

"My only hope," Grebe went on, "was to find some evidence of that in his rooms, since there was none on his person. I was lucky because Duggan Ruffins had been looking for the same thing and failed to find it.

"Here it is—hand-set printing with some of the old type in Duggan Ruffins's shop. Easily identifiable. This slip of paper will hang the man who printed it:

"'Triple Strength Capsules. To be Dissolved in any Alcoholic Liquor to Intensify its Stimulation. Guaranteed Effective and Harmless to Health.'

"And," pointed out Grebe, "to be taken on an occasion when the man who gave them was miles away. How did he get the cyanide? I'll bet you find he had to destroy a wasps' nest in his garden. If he had found this slip of paper this morning we should not have had a hope of conviction. Now it's a certainty."

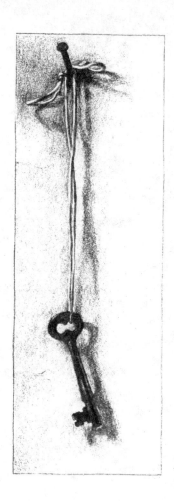

⇥**⊪⊪⊪**⊪⊷ Into Thin Air

The tall bony man with the hollow eyes was obviously in a state of great emotion when he reached Detective-Sergeant Grebe's office.

"My sister!" he said. "Disappeared!" He sank limply into the seat in front of the desk and made a helpless gesture with his hand. "Into thin air!" he added.

Grebe was skeptical about disappearances.

"Tell me what happened," he said.

"My name is Urquhart Bresson," said the tall man. "I live at Wyvely Manor.

"My sister is a maiden lady somewhat older than I. She is eccentric. Indeed very eccentric. I have been worried about her for some time. I recommended a psychiatrist in fact."

"What form did her eccentricity take?"

"She distrusted me," said Mr Bresson. "She had a great deal of money and when I suggested that I should advise her on its care she seemed

245

to resent it. She has been living in Brighton and her neighbours describe her as odd. Alone too much, perhaps.

"There was only one thing for it. I had to look after her. A sacred trust. It took me a long time to persuade her but at last she agreed to come and live here. I set aside a whole wing of the house for her. The best, the south wing. Her furniture was moved in today.

"At lunch time she arrived. She drove here from Brighton in her car, a small Austin. Characteristic of her. All that way alone at her age. I told her she ought not to have done it. There was a little argument between us but nothing of significance.

"At tea-time there was no sign of her. I went to her part of the house, but she was not there. Then I found that her car had left the garage. She had gone."

Grebe looked exasperated.

"But Mr Bresson, what in the world is extraordinary about that? She has just driven out without telling you."

Urquhart Bresson stared straight across the table.

"She hasn't!" he said excitedly. "If she had I

shouldn't have come here to report it. It is far more extraordinary than that. There is only one way out of my grounds—by the main gate. The only way up to the house is from there. There is a lodge at the gate and I employ a lodge-keeper and his wife. Most reliable people, Mr and Mrs Studd.

"The gate is kept locked. A large old-fashion-ed padlock with a single key. It was locked all today. Studd himself opened it for my sister to enter and locked it again when she had passed through. Neither he nor his wife unlocked it for her to go out. She and her car have simply vanished."

Grebe looked interested now.

"There is no place in which the car could be concealed?"

"None. The house stands in less than an acre. We have searched every inch of it. It might be possible for her to have left the pre-mises, I agree. She is . . . extraordinary enough to have done anything. Scaled the wall in some way. But her car!"

"That we shall have to find out. There is obviously some simple explanation which you have overlooked. Perhaps she had a key of the padlock of the gate unknown to you?"

"Impossible. It was an antique. I am told it must have come from some old jail. There is only one key and it has not been out of Studd's keeping for five years."

"Then they are lying. They opened it for her and have not told you."

"Equally impossible. Studd was my batman during the 1914-18 war. Been with me nearly forty years.

"It's quite impossible. The gate was never opened. But my sister with her car has gone. I must have your assistance at once. The thing must be investigated. She may have been murdered."

Grebe looked at his visitor.

"Yes," he said grimly. "I suppose it's always possible."

There was a tense silence.

"I'll come up and see the Studds," Grebe said at last.

His impression of Bill Studd and his cheerful plump wife only made the thing more puzzling. Studd was a squat square-faced man, blunt and patently honest. His wife was the kind of woman for whom the word "motherly" is always used and she justified it at once by giving Grebe a cup of tea.

"Yes, it is a funny turnout," said Studd seriously. "Miss Bresson came yesterday about midday and sounded her horn at the gate. I went out myself. I know her, of course, and she remembered me. She seemed a bit put out by the gate being locked. 'Is it always kept locked?' she asked. Then she drove in and that was the last I saw of her or her car."

"Where were you both during the afternoon?"

"Never left the lodge. I was working on a ship's model right in front of that window which overlooks the gates. But in any case no one can get through unless one of us takes the key out. Look at it."

Grebe examined a curiously wrought key and went out to see the padlock it fitted.

"Was Miss Bresson pleased to be coming here?" asked Grebe.

Studd looked a little uncomfortable. It was clear that he wanted to be loyal to his employer.

"Well, she was and she wasn't. She's a lady who has always liked her own way and Mr Bresson . . . he's on the managing side, if you know what I mean. Miss Bresson has been behaving queerly lately, we've heard, and he wanted to look after her. She wasn't a lady who liked being looked after."

"Thank you," said Grebe. "We'll come up and make a thorough search in the morning."

Grebe did so, but it seemed quite fruitless. As Bresson had said, there was only one way by which a car could enter or leave and nowhere in the grounds where one could be concealed.

Then, at the bottom of the kitchen garden, Grebe noticed the structure of an old well. He walked towards it, followed by Urquhart Bresson.

"Is this well deep?" Grebe asked.

"I don't really know. We only use it for watering. But you don't think . . . You can't suppose . . ."

"Give me any other explanation," challenged Grebe. "If a car has vanished within these walls this seems the only place in which it could be concealed. It would have been dismantled, of course."

He tested the gear and asked if there was some kind of pole handy. He was given a clothes-prop. He then instructed his young assistant to lower him.

As the bucket with Grebe went down, Bresson and Grebe's assistant watched anxiously. But there was a sound chain and a solid super-structure and Grebe reached the level of the water safely. He began to prod.

"Nothing," he called up. "There's only a few feet of water here and nothing in it. Pull me up."

He came safely to land and stood beside the others.

"Now what?" asked his assistant.

"Back to the station," said Grebe.

"But. . ." began Bresson.

"I'll communicate with you," promised Grebe, and managed to escape.

"Do you see it?" asked his assistant. "Because I'm hanged if I do."

"I think so."

"Where is she?"

"I can't tell you that. But she's where she wants to be, I think. Wait till I've made a couple of phone calls."

He was soon sitting at his office desk, his two calls made and a grin on his face.

"You seem pleased with yourself," said his assistant.

"I'm not very. I ought to have seen it at once and not gone diving down that well. Miss Bresson wasn't keen on coming. When she arrived she saw it was going to be almost a prison for her. She couldn't leave the place in her car if her brother did not let her. He started to lecture her at once for driving up alone. So when she saw a way of escape she took it."

"What way?"

"The pantechnicon, of course. Bresson said 'her furniture was moved in today.' So at least one van brought it and was leaving empty. I just phoned Studd to know the name of the removers and then phoned them. That's what happened. She gave the moving-men a few pounds, drove her car up some planks into the van and came through the lodge gates like Jonah in the whale's belly."

→❱❰← A Case For the Files

The facts of the case were almost too simple. A woman in late middle age, a Mrs Grimmets, had been set on as she walked home along a lonely road, robbed of the day's takings from her shop, and battered to death. Her body had been found in a wood, half-covered with leaves.

Mabel Grimmetts was well known in the village of Silton where she had lived since childhood. As a young girl she had married the son of the local shopkeeper, Leslie Ricks, and they had bought a small house a mile from the village, letting the accommodation over their general shop and going to it every day.

Leslie was killed in North Africa in 1941 and in 1945 Mabel married again, her second husband being a quiet and elderly clerk to an estate agent in a nearby town. Ernest Grimmetts was himself a widower and the couple, who were in their fifties when they married, were thought

255

to be in need of companionship. It was considered a most unromantic affair.

Local opinion, however, was confounded, for the two clearly felt a great deal more for each other than a convenient sort of friendship. They were seldom apart out of business hours and they spoke of each other with evident warmth and admiration. "My Mabel," Mr Grimmetts would say with a proud smile to some business associate; "My Ernest..." would begin many of Mabel's confidences in the shop. It was considered a most happy marriage.

On the day of the murder Ernest Grimmetts cycled to work as usual but, arriving home a little later than was his custom, he told Edith, the girl who worked for him and his wife, that he would not walk down to the village as he often did to meet Mabel for he expected her any minute.

His distress about this was pitiful. "If only, tonight of all nights, I had not failed my Mabel," he said, and his emotion seemed genuine. But there it was, the night was wet and windy, a typical November evening in the country, and Ernest had remained indoors warming his feet by the fire.

Mabel was last seen by George Gillman, her assistant. George had worked for her for some years, a tall, thin, not very talkative fellow in his thirties. He reported that she behaved quite normally, locking the shop door and calling good-night to him before she walked away, the takings in her handbag as usual. Investigation showed that these amounted to no more than twelve pounds.

At six o'clock, Ernest Grimmetts had become a trifle uneasy. He listened as usual to the wireless news but as soon as it was finished announced that he was going out to see what had happened to Mabel, for she had never been so late before. He set off and, according to his own account, walked to the shop without seeing any sign of his wife or of anything unusual. It occurred to him that she might have called on some neighbours, the Wades, who lived a few hundred yards nearer to the village than he did, and he retraced his steps as far as their house. When he heard that they had not seen Mabel, he returned home, but Edith informed him that Mabel still had not appeared.

It was now seven o'clock, and he decided to

telephone the police. He was diffident and apologised for giving trouble. There must, he said, be some perfectly ordinary explanation for Mabel's absence, but he thought they should be told. When he phoned later he had grown distracted and as the night passed and nothing was heard of his wife he phoned again and again and demanded that something should be done.

At nine o'clock the following morning a policeman, searching the little wood which ran along the side of the road between Mabel's shop and her home, found the body. There was evidence that it had been dragged there from the road and that a violent struggle had taken place on the roadside. The instrument, something heavy like a knob-kerrie, had not been found. The only thing discovered near the scene of the crime was an ancient and greasy cloth cap.

Detective-Sergeant Grebe checked on that. It had been made by one of the great London hatters in Edward VII's reign. They had not turned one out in that pattern since 1910.

That was all. There was not another clue to the identity of the assailant. It seemed a plain

but tragic case of robbery with violence which
—perhaps going further than the attacker intended—had ended in the woman's death.

"There are lots of cases like that," said one of
Grebe's assistants.

Grebe looked up sharply.

"Say that again," he commanded.

"I said there were lots of cases like this one."

"Just like it?"

"Of course. Women attacked and robbed."

"We're talking about murder," said Grebe.

"All right. Attacked, robbed and murdered."

"I don't think so," Grebe said. "I don't think
that even now this country has reached a point
where women can be murdered for the sake of
a few pounds and the murderer get away with
it."

His assistant seemed unconvinced.

"It will be interesting, anyhow, to see. I'm
going to have a look at the files."

Grebe was notorious in the CID for his faith in
"the files." It seemed no more than a joke to his
assistant that with a case like this to occupy
him, a case in which quick action might be of
the greatest importance, he should waste his
time looking up precedents to prove a point.

But two days later he applied for a warrant. And within three months his man was hanged.

"You see," he told his assistant, "as soon as you talked about murders like this happening every day the whole setup seemed to me suspicious. I recalled that this was precisely what I was meant to think—an ordinary little murder by some brute who would kill for a few pounds. Someone on the road, perhaps, who would wear a dirty old cloth cap.

"I didn't like it. Women don't get murdered for their handbags in England. What you remember are a few snatches and some threatening and now and again a bit of violence. They give the impression that the country's full of desperadoes but you study your statistics and you'll find that's rubbish. Someone had more motive than that for killing Mabel Grimmetts. So far from being on the spur of the minute it was a very highly-planned murder.

"Easy to follow now. Grimmetts left work a little early and instead of cycling home rode straight on down the road in which he had to meet Mabel. . .He reached a lonely point where he hid his bicycle. He had time to murder her, snatch her bag and arrive home only a little later than usual. As an auctioneer's clerk he had had an opportunity of finding among the goods to be offered at some old furniture sale the ancient cap he wore that night in case anyone should recognise him. His alibi was not cast-iron, but he did not need that, for he had built up such a reputation as a devoted husband that no one would suspect him.

"Where then, did he slip up? The answer is that he didn't—this time. He had found an excellent means of murdering his wife and making it look like an unpremeditated crime of violence by a stranger. He would probably have got away with it—*if it had been the first time.* Mr Grimmetts made the mistake of giving certainly one encore, if not more.

"Thirteen years ago a woman named Rogers, married, with no children, was killed on the way to her home from the station after she had been working in town all day. The murderer got a fiver. The husband was heartbroken. There was no arrest. But in the files was a photo of the husband. It was Grimmetts.

"There may be earlier cases. After all, Brides-in-the-Bath Smith did quite a few before someone noticed the similarity of method. What gave me the idea? Why, your saying that there were cases identical with this one. I knew that if there were, the same man was guilty in each. As, of course, he was."